"What exactly are you saying?"

Clem asked the question carefully.

Nick laughed, a sound that chilled her to the bone. "It's over. Finished. Kaput. You're a bright girl, Clemency, you know very well what I'm saying."

Clem knew, but just couldn't take it in. This was the man who'd kissed her goodbye this morning with such tenderness, such—such love. How could he be saying it was all over between them? "Are you saying you don't want me anymore, Nick?"

"No," he said savagely. "I still want you, God help me. But I'll get over that in time, never fear. There are other women in the world. But as far as you and I are concerned, that's it. From now on, just stay out of my life."

CATHERINE GEORGE was born in Wales, and following her marriage to an engineer, lived eight years in Brazil at a gold mine site, an experience she would later draw upon for her books. It was not until she and her husband returned to England and bought a village post office and general store that she submitted her first book at her husband's encouragement. Now her husband helps manage their household so that Catherine can devote more time to her writing. They have two children, a daughter and a son, who share their mother's love of language and writing.

Books by Catherine George

CATHERINE GEORGE

ever since eden

Harlequin Books

TORONTO • NEW YORK • LONDON
AMSTERDAM • PARIS • SYDNEY • HAMBURG
STOCKHOLM • ATHENS • TOKYO • MILAN

To Jacqui

Harlequin Presents first edition April 1990
ISBN 0-373-11255-6

Original hardcover edition published in 1989
by Mills & Boon Limited

CHAPTER ONE

THE MIDSUMMER moon shone, bright and obliging, just as if hired for the occasion. It silvered the grass and painted black pools of shadow under the trees in the gardens of Overbury Manor, while inside the old house chandeliers glittered down on a ballroom scene straight from a precocious child's fantasy. Masked characters from every fairy-tale ever read pranced and perspired to the heavy beat of the latest hit: Red Riding Hood and the Pied Piper, Snow White and a selection of Dwarfs, Hansel and Gretel, Jack and Jill, Goldilocks and innumerable Bears were all cavorting on the dance-floor, roaring at each other's antics, everyone having a wonderful time. The only exception seemed to be the lady who should, by right, have been enjoying the ball most.

A tall, brocaded Cinderella, with powdered ringlets and gilt satin mask, stood at bay near one of the long open windows, resentment in every line of her as she parried three men who hemmed her in like dogs snarling over a bone. As Prince Charming grew more proprietorial, and Sinbad and Robin Hood more predatory, a hint of desperation edged the smile the lady turned on her three admirers.

'By the way,' said Cinderella, inspired, 'how was the hundred-share index at close of trading today?'

No magic wand could have worked faster. In an instant the three men were deep in discussion of share prices and the world market, and not one of them even noticed when Cinderella drifted, retreating, until she could make her escape through the nearest window. Once on the terrace she lifted up her panniered skirts and raced down the shallow stone steps, threading her way swiftly through the knot garden, then on down an avenue of beeches until she found the opening she was looking for. With a swift look over her shoulder, she turned off on a narrow path which brought her to a copse of trees near an artificial lake, and with a sigh of relief she reached the sanctuary of a wrought-iron seat which was hidden, as remembered, by a thick screen of conifers.

She sank down on the seat and leaned back against the hard iron tracery, kicking off slippers sewn with beads to represent the necessary glass. As she gazed over the gleaming stretch of water she began to feel better, smiling as a ray of moonlight lit up the frivolous little gazebo on the far bank of the lake. As a child she had come here often to fêtes and garden parties. The gardens, particularly, had always been a favourite haunt, full of secret places for a child to play. She sighed. In some ways it had been a mistake to revisit the place tonight, to see it full of inebriated strangers. But Hugo had been very insistent. The ball was for charity, and a lot of useful people would be there. Useful to Hugo Barrington, he meant; contacts who could help him up the financial ladder he was climbing with such determination. Besides, as he had pointed out several times, the venue was Overbury Manor, hired out regularly these days for banquets and balls, and near enough to Clem's parents' home to make an overnight stay there at the weekend far more convenient than driving back to London after the ball.

Clem flicked at her elaborate skirts with distaste. She loathed this kind of costume affair. Her own idea of fancy dress was raiding the trunks in the attic at home to play Charades with her sisters, parading in Granny's flapper dresses, or fashioning weird and wonderful costumes from crêpe paper and faded artificial flowers. Her present outfit was stiff and uncomfortable, and she eased the bodice away from her heated skin, grateful for the cool night air coming off the water.

She smiled as she remembered the argument with Hugo over their choice of characters. He had been quite obstinate, obviously rather fancying himself as Prince Charming. And to be fair, she conceded, the style suited him well enough. The powdered wig concealed the slight thinning of his hair, and the velvet coat was flattering, but if she were honest his legs were a bit on the spindly side for silk stockings and knee-breeches. Her own plea to dress as Cinders in rags with soot on her face had been summarily quashed. Hugo wanted her as Cinderella dressed for the ball, the Princess Incognita herself, and had been unusually eager to lash out for once, paying a large, unspecified sum for the hire of the elaborate costumes he insisted were necessary. Clem wondered idly if he'd recoup his outlay in the contacts he expected to make. From her own point of view she felt she'd more than done her bit towards it. For two hours she'd smiled and chatted and charmed as Hugo wanted, playing her part dutifully right up to the point where Robin Hood and his chum had demanded dances with her. Then Sinbad's hands had been hot and damp, Robin Hood over-blunt with his opinions of her charms, and as far as Cinderella was concerned they could both jump in the lake. She smiled. It was a great idea, but on second thoughts no. She wanted the lake to herself. En route to her hiding place she had passed quite a few people strolling in the moonlight near the house, but happily no one had penetrated this far.

She yawned and settled herself more comfortably on the seat, her eyes dreamy as she gazed out over the water. The music from the ballroom was just faintly audible, sounding rather pleasant from this distance, but she had no intention of returning yet to the heat and noise inside. It was so much pleasanter to sit alone out here in the garden, enjoying the rare pleasure of a perfect summer night. The charity organisers were no doubt delirious with joy over their luck with the weather, particularly with a full moon thrown in as the crowning touch. It seemed a shame to waste it all indoors.

A twig cracked nearby and Clem waited, resigned. It had been only a matter of time before Hugo put in an appearance, of course, but to her dismay Clem realised she didn't want him to find her. Which was an unsettling thought, since until tonight she had been giving due consideration to the idea of marrying him one day. Which was the point at issue, of course. If he were the right man, she knew very well no consideration of any kind would come into it. Something her sisters had demonstrated very conclusively in their choice of husbands.

There was a slight rustle in the copse, and she frowned.

'Hugo?' she called uncertainly, peering through the darkness. 'Is that you?' She caught a glimpse of satin knee-breeches, brocaded coat, a wink of light from shoe-buckles, as a tall figure materialised in the shadows, a tricorne hat hiding his face as he made an elaborate leg from a distance.

'Alas,' he said, in an oddly muffled voice, 'I confess I'm not the fortunate Hugo. He of the red velvet coat and powdered wig, I presume? Your Prince Charming.' The intruder retreated to lean against a tree, his upper half hidden from her in the shadows.

Clem stayed where she was, wondering if she

should make a run for it, yet not in the least afraid. She eyed the figure in the shadows curiously, deciding no menace came from him, despite the aura of mystery.

'That's the one. Are you by any chance Prince Charming, too?'

'No, Highness. Mine is a different story.' There was a hint of laughter in the muffled voice. 'Unfortunately my partner was prevented from coming at the eleventh hour. So here I am—alone.'

Clem's eyes gleamed at him through the slits of her mask. 'Is that why you're out here in the garden instead of inside, dancing?'

'No. I find dancing difficult at the moment. Especially what passes for dancing among the young these days.'

'Are you so very old, then?'

'Centuries old, Highness!'

'Only two centuries, by your costume, sir.'

'And are you an expert on costume?'

'Interested, rather than expert.' Clem peered at the stranger, intrigued, wishing he'd come nearer. 'Do you know Overbury Manor?' she asked.

'Yes. My parents live in the district.' He laughed a little. 'But that's not why I'm here in the garden. I followed *you*, Highness. I'd been watching you from a vantage point behind a pillar on the other side of the ballroom, saw you fending off your three predators——'

'Two predators, one protector, to be exact.'

'From where I was standing the difference was indistinguishable. You had the air of a graceful doe keeping three rutting stags at bay. Then I saw you say something to them, and Abracadabra, your suitors were knee-deep in conversation with each other instead. How did you do it?'

Clem's mouth curved in a mischievous smile. 'Magic!'

'If you mean you're a bewitching creature, Cinderella, I'm in full agreement.'

She narrowed her eyes at this. 'It was all too easy. I said the magic words "share prices", and the spell was cast.'

The stable stock in the distance chimed midnight, and the man gave another muffled laugh.

'The witching hour. Time to unmask.'

'And time I went back to the ball,' said Clem briskly, searching for a slipper.

Before she could find it the man moved towards her and went down on one knee, his head bent as he rescued the slipper and slid it on her foot. She felt his fingers fleetingly on her instep, and caught her lower lip in her teeth, breathless as she gazed down on the satin-clad shoulders and black three-cornered hat. The desire to see the stranger's face was suddenly overpowering.

'Will you unmask if I do?' she asked.

'If you really want me to.' The tall man rose to his full height and removed his hat. Clem gasped, a hand to her throat as the moonlight revealed the stranger in every detail.

From his buckled shoes to the foaming lace of his cravat, her companion was the archetypal eighteenth-century exquisite. But from the throat upwards he wore the mask of some apocryphal cat-like beast, with slanting openings for his eyes to gleam through, and delicate, irrelevant tusks above the aperture which allowed his own white teeth to show through the dark silky hair which covered his entire face and head.

He swept her a bow. 'I *said* I came from a different tale, Highness. Mask or no mask, *you* can only be Beauty, while I—allow me to introduce myself—am the Beast.' And he straightened, laughing his hollow, muffled laugh inside his mask.

Clem stood up, shaking out her skirts as her heartbeat slowed gradually to normal. 'No doubt you took pleasure in that, Sir Beast. Do you enjoy frightening defenceless females?'

He stood very still, then shook his fantastic head. 'No, Highness, I've no stomach for it at all. Which, in part, is why I chose to wear the mask.'

'Are you so ugly, then?'

'Beauty lives in the eye of the beholder, so they say.' He shrugged. 'To my mother I'm not ugly. Others—others might think differently.'

Silence fell between them once more, as the two brocade-clad figures faced each other by the moonlit lake.

'In the story,' Clem heard herself say, 'a kiss changed the Beast into a mortal man.' And on impulse she reached up and kissed the place where the silky dark hair covered his cheek. She sensed the sudden rigidity in the stranger, and stepped back, her face warm behind the mask as she gestured towards him in appeal. She watched, expectant, as two slim hands went up in what seemed like slow motion, the lace ruffles at his wrists falling back as he loosened the mask at the throat. She held her breath, her curiosity almost outweighed by fear of what the mask might hide. Was he so ugly, or deformed, even? It was possible his reasons for hiding his face had been a lot stronger than a mere whim to assume the role of Beast for a fancy-dress ball.

She waited in silence as he slowly peeled the mask upwards, to reveal an aggressive chin, a wide lower lip and a short, curving upper lip, a jutting nose and high, sharply chiselled cheekbones—but only one visible eye. The other was hidden by a black patch. And as the mask came off the man shook back his hair and moved deliberately so that the cruel white light fell on one half of his face, showing up an angry scar which began just above the jawline and travelled upwards, disappearing under the eye-patch to re-emerge on its journey to his hairline.

Clem's reactions were mixed, but the strongest was relief, and she gazed very steadily at the face of the stranger, aware of a strong feeling of recognition, certain she had met him before. 'You've been hurt,' she said with compassion. 'Is that why you wore the mask?'

His smile matched the mockery in his voice. 'Because of my vanity, you mean.'

'No. I think you're probably over-conscious of the scar. You needn't be.' She tilted her head to one side, assessing him dispassionately. 'And the patch is rather romantic, I think.'

'What's underneath it isn't.'

'Have you lost your eye?'

'No. Somehow or other it survived. I'm assured I'll even be able to use it again in time.'

'Was it an accident?'

'Yes.' He ran his hand impatiently through his hair. 'Let's not talk about it, please. Instead, Highness, I think you should repay the compliment. It's time you played fair and let me see what lies beneath *your* mask.'

Clem swept him a curtsy and did as he asked, smiling up at him as her mask dangled by its ribbons from her hand. 'Better?'

He looked at her for several moments in silence, then smiled a strange, slow smile. 'I was mistaken. It would have been much more like fair play if you'd kept the mask on. You're very beautiful, Highness.'

'Moonlight is kind.'

'Then God help me when we meet in daylight —one way and another.' His face looked haggard suddenly, then he took one of her hands and raised it to his lips, the single penetrating glance meeting hers over it. 'Do you want to go in now?'

Clem did not. She wanted nothing more than to stay exactly where she was. 'Do you?' she parried.

His fingers tightened on hers. 'If a man finds he's strayed into a fairy-tale, complete with beautiful princess in the moonlight, is he likely to want it to end?'

'In that case I suggest we sit here for a while.' She resumed her seat on the iron bench, patting the place beside her. 'Let's watch the moonlight move over the lake and pretend we're old friends who do this sort of thing all the time.'

He sat down beside her with alacrity, and stretched out legs which were very much suited to silk stockings and satin knee-breeches. Not spindly at all, Clem noted with approval. Her companion was on the thin side, possibly, but muscular and fairly tall. Quite a few inches taller than herself, which was by no means common. Most men met her eye to eye, or fell short. Hugo was a fraction taller, it was true, but not much.

'Since we're old friends,' said the man abruptly, 'we should have no trouble in finding things to talk about. What subjects would please you, Highness?'

'Ourselves?'

'Right. You start.' Very gently he took possession of her hand, then leaned back, looking down at her with an encouraging smile.

Clem smiled back and obediently gave him a few basic details, telling him she designed and made clothes in partnership with a friend from art school days, had two sisters and one brother, came originally from a village near Monmouth, and currently shared a small terraced house in Putney with two other girls. 'There,' she concluded. 'One potted history. Now it's your turn.'

'Not so fast! You haven't told me your name.'
His eye gleamed down at her. 'Unless you prefer to
remain as Princess Incognita?'

'Since it wasn't my idea in the first place, certainly not. My name's Vaughan—Clemency Vaughan.'

'Clemency!' He laughed, a husky, infectious
sound she responded to instinctively. 'And *are* you
merciful, Miss Vaughan?'

'I hope I would be if necessary.'

'And this Hugo—Prince Charming back there.'
He raised the hand he held to peer at her fingers.
'No badge of ownership yet. Will you allow him to
buy you one?'

'If you mean a ring, I don't regard one as a badge
of ownership,' she said. 'If ever a man *does* put a
ring on my finger, it will be as a token of
partnership, Sir Beast.'

'Ah! A latter-day Cinderella. I apologise, and
agree wholeheartedly.' He hesitated. 'Do you
require chapter and verse from me now,
Clemency?'

She shrugged. 'Only as much as you wish. Or
you can preserve your anonymity altogether, if you
prefer. I don't suppose we'll meet again.'

'Why shouldn't we? Unless you find this face of
mine a bit hard to take, of course.' His voice was so
carefully expressionless, Clem experienced a sudden impulse to kiss his scar, tell him it didn't matter in the least to her, or to anyone else worth
knowing.

'As I said before,' she stated matter-of-factly, 'the

patch *and* the scar are probably assets, where my sex is concerned. Females are usually bowled over by the piratical look.'

'Some, possibly.' He raised her hand to his lips again. 'Allow me to tell you what a very lovely lady you are, Clemency Vaughan. In more ways than just that beautiful face.'

Clem was glad of the neutralising moonlight, as colour rushed to her face. 'Why, thank you, kind sir. But I can't just go on calling you "sir". Won't you tell me *your* name? Or is it classified information?'

'No, very ordinary. Wood—Nicholas. Nick to my friends.'

She frowned as she sensed tension again in the man beside her. 'Sounds familiar, ' she said slowly, then turned to him, smiling. 'The people who organised the ball! Hugo said their name was Wood.'

He laughed, relaxed again. 'True. Otherwise wild horses wouldn't have dragged me here. My aunt is a small but very overpowering lady, and passionately devoted to charitable concerns, so here I am as commanded, but without Miss Melanie Wood in tow. My sister,' he added, shaking his head. 'Eighteen and a handful.'

'So why didn't she turn up?'

'It was a matter of costume. My scar and I are not what you might call used to each other yet, so my attendance was conditional on a suitable disguise, thus Mel as Beauty and me as the Beast.'

'What happened?'

'I was rash enough to leave hiring the costumes

to her, the little monkey. Mine arrived as planned, but when Miss Melanie put in an appearance my father almost had a stroke. She'd changed her mind, she said. It was too hot for all that brocade.' Nicholas Wood laughed. 'She tripped downstairs in her version of the Little Mermaid, which meant a skin-tight gold tail, long blonde wig and a few pearls scattered strategically over her top half. My mother took one look and sent her up to her room mid-tantrum, and I, bloody fool that I am, obediently came on alone.'

'Are you sorry you did?' Clem flushed hotly the moment the words left her mouth, certain he'd think she was angling for a compliment.

'Don't be embarrassed. I know what you meant.' His intuition surprised her. 'And how could I be sorry? If we never meet again, Highness, I shall have this interlude to look back on.' He put a finger under her chin and turned her face towards him, his wide mouth turning up irresistibly at the corners. 'May I ask a final boon before Prince Charming comes after you in hot pursuit?'

'What is it?'

'Since I took off my disguise at your request—very reluctantly, I may add—will you return the compliment and let me see you without your wig?'

Clem's eyes opened wide, then she began to laugh as she shook her head. 'Sorry, can't be done. It may look like horsehair to you, Nicholas Wood, but it's mine, every last hair of it thick with powder because I wouldn't *wear* a wig.'

He caught a ringlet in either hand and pulled gently, bringing her face close to his. He breathed in sharply. 'A man can only take so much,' he muttered huskily, and kissed her.

Clem sat very still for a moment, taken by surprise, then she melted willingly into arms that closed about her in welcome, and her own arms went up around his neck. Their lips parted in unison as he held her so tightly against him that she could feel him trembling a little, his heartbeat thudding against her own, affecting her in a way she had never experienced before. At his touch, the feeling of recognition surged back again, along with a multitude of others clamouring inside her. She was sure she had never met this man before, yet she felt she knew him just the same, knew the touch of his hands and mouth, the feel of his body against hers as she experienced at last, for the very first time, the true heat of an answering flame in her own blood. She pulled away from him a little, her eyes glittering into his.

'I had no idea!' she said, in a strange, stifled voice, and held up her mouth again, and Nicholas Wood took it with a helpless groan, crushing her to him as he kissed her in a way she responded to with delight. Clem freed her mouth at last, but only to move her lips with exquisite care over the scar, pulling down his head so she could follow the raised ridge of it up into his thick black hair.

Suddenly an angry voice shattered their idyll. Clem jumped away guiltily, her hand to her mouth as Hugo's voice sounded in the distance, shouting her name.

'I must go,' she gasped, and held up her face for one last kiss.

Nicholas Wood held her fast for a moment, staring down grimly into her upturned face. 'Prince Charming—is he important?'

'No.' Her eyes widened as the truth of it struck her. 'No, he's not. But I don't want him to spoil this——'

'Give me your telephone number.'

'Will you remember it?' she asked anxiously, and he nodded, repeating it after her until he was satisfied he knew it.

'I'll ring you soon. Very soon.' He kissed her again, fiercely, then let her go. Clem gathered up her skirt to run in the direction of Hugo's voice, gave the tall, dark figure in the shadows a last smile over her shoulder and forced herself to leave him standing there alone, watching her out of sight.

'Where in God's name have you been?' demanded Hugo as she glided into view through the line of beeches. 'I was ready to ring the police!'

'I've been sitting by the lake, looking at the moonlight on the water,' said Clem, unrepentant. 'It was stifling in the ballroom, and you were so immersed in the Stock Market I decided to take a stroll in the fresh air.'

Hugo was deeply affronted, and insisted she stayed on at the dance for an hour longer than intended by way of reparation, then spent the entire journey to her parents' home telling her how irresponsibly she'd behaved, and how embarrassing it had been to make excuses to his friends for her disappearance. None of it had the least effect on his companion. She sat beside him in dreamy silence all the way home, deaf to his complaints, all her attention turned inward on the picture in her mind of Beauty and the Beast beside a moonlit lake, and of those few startlingly passionate kisses which made her heart thump at the mere memory of them, and left her on fire for more. When Hugo drew up outside the Vaughan home in Llanhowell it was two in the morning and the house was quiet, but lights were on in the kitchen for the latecomers' return.

A thermos of coffee and a plate of sandwiches waited for them on the table, and Clem gestured towards them politely, smothering a yawn.

'Do help yourself, Hugo, if you want. I won't keep you company—I'm for bed.'

'Have you nothing to say by way of apology?' he demanded, looking faintly ridiculous as he bristled in his velvet jacket and knee-breeches, which looked odd now he'd discarded the wig and wore his usual black lace-ups instead of the silver buckles of Prince Charming.

Clem fought back laughter in favour of smiling penitence, but it was difficult when excitement blazed inside her like a forest fire.

'I apologise for worrying you, Hugo, but I was perfectly safe. I know the garden at Overbury Manor almost as well as the one out there.' She gestured towards the window. 'I lost track of the time, that's all. I'm sorry.'

Hugo munched on a sandwich, looking irritable. 'It looked so bad to the others, Clemency. Surely you realise that!'

She looked hard at him. 'Was that all that mattered to you?'

He had the grace to look uncomfortable. 'No, no, of course not. But you just don't seem to realise anything could have happened to you out there in the dark on your own.'

Something had, she thought, hugging her secret to herself. She smiled at him with a radiance he eyed with suspicion.

'But nothing bad *could* have happened to me out there, Hugo. We were fairy-tale characters, remember. Fairy-tales always have happy endings.'

Hugo looked unappeased. 'I only hope you didn't spoil that dress.'

Clem swept him an ironic obeisance, then revolved in front of him slowly, holding out her rose brocade skirts. 'I don't think so. All present and correct—or pure and unspotted, whichever you prefer.' She glided over to the door, then turned and smiled at him mischievously. 'By the way, I'm so glad you vetoed my idea of a sooty Cinders.'

He frowned at her suspiciously. 'Really? Why?'

'If I *had* been in rags with a dirty face I would have been in quite the wrong fairy-tale after all, as things turned out.' She remembered something. 'By the way, I'd like to make a start back for town straight after breakfast, if it's all right with you.'

'But I thought we were staying to lunch!' Hugo

looked more aggrieved than ever.

Clem shook her head. 'I have to get back. I'm expecting a very important phone-call later in the day.'

'One of Lady Robina's friends with an order, I suppose.' He shrugged huffily, and poured himself a cup of coffee.

'No, nothing at all like that. No business involved, just pleasure.' She grinned at his incensed glare, and floated up to bed to lie for hours thinking how she had very nearly missed meeting Nicholas Wood beside the lake at Overbury Manor. If she'd followed her own inclination and refused to give in to Hugo's demands about attending the charity ball, she might have gone through life never knowing what it was like to fall in love. Her eyes opened wide in the darkness at the thought. Were a few stolen moments in the moonlight all it took to fall in love? It hardly seemed probable. She was twenty-eight years old, she reminded herself, not an impressionable teenager, old enough to know that what seemed like gilt in the moonlight might rub off the gingerbread all too quickly when she met her fairy-tale lover in the prosaic light of everyday. *If* she met him. How could she be certain Nicholas would remember her number, or ring her even if he did? But none of her arguments did anything at all to reduce the shining certainty that tonight had been the most momentous occasion of her life. Clem fell asleep at last, serene in the belief that not only was Nicholas Wood the mate she'd been waiting for all her life, but that, by some miracle, his feelings for her were exactly the same.

CHAPTER TWO

THE JOURNEY to London next day was not the pleasantest one Clem had ever made. It rained all the way along the M4, Hugo was in a very sour mood, and Clem too taken up with her own thoughts to try to sweeten his temper as she would have done on most other occasions. The sun reappeared as they reached the Hammersmith fly-over, and by the time Hugo stopped the car in the quiet little terrace in Putney midsummer was in full swing again. Clem's spirits soared as she jumped out of the black BMW.

'Thank you, Hugo,' she said, and hoisted her overnight case from the back seat. 'Don't get out—I can manage.'

Hugo stared at her in affront. 'Aren't you going to ask me in?'

'Not this time, if you don't mind. The girls may not even be decent yet, and I don't suppose there's much in the house to eat.'

'Then let's go somewhere for lunch,' he said promptly.

Clem shook her head. 'Not today.' She eyed him for a moment, thinking it over, then changed her mind. 'On the other hand, perhaps it might be as well. Let me just dash in the house for a moment—wait there, I won't be long.'

24

She flew up the path past the tiny patch of lawn and the rowan tree, her fingers unsteady as she put her key in the door. One of her fellow tenants, Emma Reeves, stood in the kitchen in a sketchy top and shorts, stirring something in a saucepan. She smiled warmly in greeting at Clem, then peered round her suspiciously.

'Hi! Hugo isn't with you, I hope?'

'No, he's out in the car. Why? Any phone calls?'

Emma tut-tutted. 'What *have* you been up to, Clemency Vaughan? As a matter of fact, yes. Someone with a dark brown voice, name of Nick. Said he'd ring back about six.'

Clem threw her arms round Emma's sturdy little person and hugged her so hard the other girl begged for mercy. 'Thanks, Em. That's just what I wanted to hear! I'm off down to the Drummond on the corner of the High Street for something to eat with Hugo——' She looked at her watch. 'Should be home by two at the latest, just in case Nick rings again before I'm back.'

Emma whistled. 'Is he likely to?'

'No idea—but I'm not taking any chances.'

'If you're that anxious, why don't you share this rather peculiar risotto with me and just tell Hugo to push off?'

Clem shook her head. 'Don't tempt me! But I'd better have a talk with Hugo before—well, before.'

Emma's eyes glistened with curiosity, then she laughed as an impatient toot sounded on the BMW's horn outside. 'Off you go, then. I'll keep this mysterious Nick on the boil if he rings before you're back.'

Clem found it very difficult to embark on the conversation she had decided was necessary as far as Hugo was concerned. It was by no means the first time she'd let a man down gently, but with Hugo the reason was vastly different from all the other times, and she felt guilty. Until the evening before, she had been more or less contemplating marriage with Hugo Barrington, and had an idea he was fully aware of the fact. Yet it had taken only a few brief moments with the unknown Nicholas Wood to make the idea unthinkable. Even if she never saw Nick again it would make no difference now. Just meeting him had rendered a relationship with anyone else out of the question.

She knew in her heart of hearts that her reason for encouraging Hugo had been her feeling that time was passing, that she was twenty-eight, and high time she settled down if she wanted a home and children. As she did. And Hugo seemed like solid husband material: ambitious, suitable, even comfortably off financially. But now everything was changed. And, after a few mouthfuls of a salad she didn't want, Clem began, with care, to let Hugo know there was no point in going on with their relationship. He almost choked on a mouthful of pasta, his face flushing hectically under his smooth sandy hair as he stared at her.

'*What*? You don't know what you're saying!'

She swallowed some wine, feeling wretched. 'A clean break is better, Hugo, than letting you think——'

'Letting me think what?' he interrupted swiftly, his lips thinning. 'I've never asked you to marry me.'

'True. But lately you seem to have taken it for granted we were moving towards *some* kind of permanent relationship.'

Hugo had himself well in hand almost at once. He refilled his wineglass and sat back, smiling at her loftily. 'Well, yes, I'll admit I had toyed with the idea of asking you to move in with me. But marriage—that's a different kettle of fish. I'd have to be very sure any bride I chose was eligible in every way; well-connected socially. Nothing against your family, of course,' he added hastily, 'but a doctor with a country practice can hardly be termed a useful connection in my line of business.'

Clem's eyes narrowed to a cold sapphire glitter. 'How upsetting for my father to find he falls short of your requirements as a social connection! Not that it matters, of course, since the question doesn't arise.' She thrust her glass at him. 'I think I'll have a little more wine, then we can go our separate ways—in peace.'

Hugo looked a little shamefaced. 'Your problem, Clem,' he said sulkily, 'is that all the warmth is on the outside, on that beautiful exterior of yours. Inside you're cold.'

After the events of the night before, Clem knew beyond any doubt he was mistaken. 'You're entitled to your opinion, of course. But you're quite wrong, as it happens.'

'I suppose you're referring to the chap you lived

with once.'

Her eyes fell to hide the guilty surprise in them. She had actually forgotten Evan. Evan Rees, the graphic designer she'd first met in college, the one who had persuaded her to share the house in Putney with him at a very vulnerable time in her life. Wild, talented Evan, with his passion for mountains, had climbed one too many and fallen to his death on the anniversary of their first year together. But that was a long time ago. It seemed like light years away. And a lot of water had flowed under Putney Bridge since then.

'He's the reason really, isn't he?' demanded Hugo, leaning forward. 'Just because you got hurt once, you fight shy of letting yourself get involved again.'

It seemed wisest to allow him to labour under his quite mistaken delusion; kinder than telling him she'd met someone else. At the mere thought of the someone else in question Clem's heart beat faster, and she got to her feet, unable to sit still any longer. Hugo rose with her, but she shook her head.

'Please, stay and finish your lunch. I'll make my own way back.'

He looked at her glumly, then shrugged. 'If that's what you want.'

'It is, Hugo.' Clem held out a hand, and after a moment, reluctantly, he took it. 'No hard feelings?'

To his credit, he managed a smile. 'You ask a lot, Clem. But—well, all right. No hard feelings. Perhaps we might have lunch together one day.'

'Yes, let's.' She leaned forward and kissed his

cheek. 'And thank you for taking me to the ball last night, Hugo. I wouldn't have missed it for the world.'

His eyebrows rose. 'While I, Cinderella, have a feeling the entire evening was a colossal mistake on my part.'

She patted his cheek, smiling, and with a last goodbye made for the door, oblivious of the usual swivelling male heads as she passed on her way out of Hugo Barrington's life.

When she got home she found Emma out in the small back garden, surrounded by the Sunday papers as she lay mopping up the sun.

'No, he hasn't rung,' she said, grinning, before Clem could say a word. 'The telephone has remained quite, quite mute. He *did* say six, you know.'

Clem smiled sheepishly. 'Just checking. Where's Jane?'

'Staying overnight with the future in-laws.' Emma stretched luxuriously. 'Get your clothes off and come and join me—this sun's gorgeous. Besides, I think I merit a blow-by-blow account of what actually went on last night, Cinderella.'

'You'll never believe it!' Clem laughed, and ran upstairs to change, reappearing presently in a faded blue running vest and striped shorts, her hair tied up on top of her head. While she smeared herself liberally with suntan cream she gave Emma most of the details of the ball, going on at length about the meeting with Nick in the moonlight, but omitting any mention of the kisses, which proved too private to share with anyone.

Emma's eyes goggled at the point where Clem's intruder in her hidden retreat proved to be the fairy-tale Beast. 'You're kidding!'

Clem assured her she was not.

'But didn't he scare you to death out there on your own?'

'No. I was a bit startled at first, but not really frightened. I knew from the first he meant me no harm.'

'No—well, I mean, if someone had assault or rape in mind, I suppose they'd hardly get themselves up in fancy dress to do it. A mask, yes, but not lace and knee-breeches and so on.' Emma shook her head and sighed. 'And to think *my* Saturday night was spent at the cinema, watching Woody Allen with Hamish.'

'And very nice, too!' Clem lay flat on her back with her face to the sun, and finished her story in response to her friend's urging.

There was silence afterwards, then Emma said slowly, 'So on the strength of a few minutes in the moonlight with a man you've never met before in your life you've broken off with Hugo Barrington, boy wonder of the City.' She chuckled. 'And there I was, afraid you were actually working up to marrying him one day!'

'Afraid?'

'Yes. Now it's all over, I can say I'm sure it would never have worked, Clem. A bit lacking in the humour department, our Hugo.'

'I suppose you're right,' said Clem, thinking it over. She sighed. 'Poor Hugo! He turned a bit nasty at first, but by the time we parted he was being rather sporting.' Suddenly she leapt to her feet as the telephone rang, and tore into the house, out of breath as she grabbed the receiver.

'It's only me,' said her mother. 'Your father tends to be restless until he knows you're back safely.'

'Mother, I'm sorry!' said Clem, stricken. 'No excuse—I just forgot. My mind was rather full of having told Hugo we should go our separate ways.'

'So that's why you were so abstracted this morning. I wondered why you wouldn't stay for lunch.' Angharad Vaughan sounded amused. 'And what was wrong with Hugo, then? He's lasted longer than some.'

'Nothing, really. The fault's with me, I suppose.'

'Not as far as your loving mother's concerned, Clemency Vaughan. You just haven't found the right man yet, that's all.'

It seemed precipitate to announce that she was sure she had, so Clem just laughed and asked if the usual Sunday hotline had been busy with calls from her sisters, and learned that Kit's two small sons had German measles, and Charity was proud to announce she was pregnant for the third time.

'I had a feeling she was. Isn't it a bit soon?'

Mrs Vaughan laughed. 'Luiza's three, Dolly's five, and Charity feels it's high time she gave her husband a son.'

'How about Penry? He hasn't been round lately.'

'Cutting a swathe through the nurses at the hospital—as usual.'

Clem went back to the garden and stretched out again. 'It was only Mother,' she said, sighing.

'It's not four yet, dummy. The man said six.' Emma eyed the tense, graceful figure lying beside her. 'I've never seen you like this before. You're like a cat on hot bricks.'

Clem agreed ruefully, and did her best to relax, applying herself to the Sunday papers and making as intelligent an attempt at conversation as possible for someone whose mind was in a frenzy of anticipation at the thought of the expected phone call. When Emma went indoors to make tea, Clem gave up all pretence at doing anything but daydreaming about the night before as the sun poured down on the sheltered square of lawn. Nature had been generous, giving her an olive-tinted skin which tanned easily, and she lay motionless, acquiring a deeper shade of gold as the afternoon wore on, all her concentration on the hope of hearing that deep, clear-cut voice again. Tea had been drunk, Emma had wandered off for a bath, and still there was an hour to be lived through until six. Clem was amazed at herself. She knew she was behaving like a schoolgirl with a first crush, but no amount of self-derision had the slightest effect. As the minutes ticked by her nerves frankly jangled, until the tension inside her became almost unbearable.

Just before five-thirty the telephone rang, and she flew to answer it, her hand shaking as she picked up the receiver.

'Hello,' she said huskily, and sagged against the

wall as she heard the longed-for voice.

'Clemency?'

'Yes.'

'Nick. I know I told your friend I'd ring at six, but I just couldn't hang on any longer.'

'I'm glad. Neither could I.' She heard him breathe in sharply.

'What's your address?' he demanded.

She told him and he chuckled, the sound of his unconcealed delight raising goose-bumps along her spine. 'If I come round in half an hour would you come out with me for a meal? Please?'

Clem's eyes opened wide. 'Half an hour! Why, where are you?'

'Parson's Green.'

She laughed unsteadily. 'You mean we're almost neighbours?'

'Amazing, isn't it? Well, will you come?'

'Hold on.' She put a hand over the receiver as Emma came down the stairs in one of her prettiest dresses. 'Are you going out, Em?'

'I told you. *Twice,*' said Emma severely. 'Hamish is taking me to a party in Maidenhead. I knew you weren't paying attention.'

Clem pulled a face. 'Sorry. When will you be back?'

Emma grinned. 'Late—very late, if you like. And did you take in the fact that Jane isn't coming back at all tonight? She's going straight to the office in the morning from Guildford.'

Clem blew an ecstatic kiss at her friend, then took her hand from the mouthpiece. 'Hello? Nick?'

'I thought you'd rung off.'

'No fear. Could you make it an hour?'

'If I must. But not a second more.'

Clem put down the telephone in a daze of delight, her face flushed and radiant.

'Wow!' said Emma in awe. 'This man must be something. That *was* him, I imagine.'

'Yes!' Clem seized her friend and did a war-dance round the cramped little hall. 'Would you believe it, Em, he lives in Parsons's Green, and he'll be here in an hour——Oh God, I'm a mess, what can I wear? And just look at my hair——'

'Calm down!' Emma rubbed an elbow irritably. 'You've bumped me into the banisters, you idiot. Honestly, Clem, I've never seen you like this before.'

'I've never been like this before.' Clem took a deep, steadying breath. 'I've just *got* to get myself together.'

Emma hauled her into the kitchen and opened the refrigerator. 'I assume you want to feed this man here. Look, there's half a cold chicken I roasted yesterday, some salad greens, cheese. And you can open this wine Hamish brought me last night.'

'Em, you're a miracle!'

'I know. Now, for pity's sake go and stand under a cold shower and recite your twelve times table until you're sane. Works wonders.'

They both jumped at the thunderous knock at the front door.

'I don't know why Hamish can't ring the bell like everyone else,' said Emma, resigned, and patted

Clem on the cheek. 'I'll go straight off, love, otherwise he's quite likely to insist on waiting to see if this Nick of yours merits the Hamish Munroe gold seal of approval.'

Clem raced upstairs before the door closed behind Emma, lingering only long enough under the shower to rinse the last traces of the previous night's powder from her hair. She dried the springy curls at frantic speed while she decided what to wear, worried that Nick would probably find her everyday clothes a bit of a let-down after her fancy-dress finery. Her taste was fairly conservative, and ran to fine materials she made up herself in the plain styles she preferred, and after much indecision she finally stayed with a beautifully cut lawn dress, printed in shades of kingfisher and indigo which accentuated the tan of her bare arms and throat, the skirt cut to float gracefully as she moved.

After applying a minimum of make-up to her face, Clem thrust her fingers through her still damp hair and ran downstairs to set the table. The small dining-room was separated by an archway from the bay-windowed 'parlour', as Emma liked to call it, and Clem spread the best linen cloth on the table, and ran into the garden for a handful of buds from the Iceberg roses just coming into bloom. Arranged in a small crystal jug, they added a festive touch to the everyday cutlery and wineglasses, and, feeling this was an extra-special occasion, she rummaged for a pair of unused candles in the kitchen drawer, and put them on a couple of Coalport saucers kept for use as ashtrays.

At top speed she carved chicken and washed lettuce and radicchio, then whisked up some French dressing, quite amazed by her own efficiency in the circumstances, since her hands were obliged to work in conjuction with a mind inclined to wander every other minute to matters far less mundane than mere food.

When the doorbell rang at exactly the appointed time, Clem froze for a second, then breathed in deeply and ran to open the door, smiling in radiant welcome at the tall figure silhouetted against the evening sun.

'My God,' said Nicholas Wood, his voice husky with awe. 'Are you real?'

'Pinch me and see for yourself,' she said happily, suddenly in command of herself for the first time in hours. She beckoned him inside with ceremony. 'Welcome to my humble abode, sir.'

Nick followed her into the hall and closed the door, standing with his back against it as he looked at her in silence, his eyes travelling from her bare, sandalled feet to the unruly mane of ash-fair hair.

Clem returned the look with interest, wondering why a plain white shirt and cream cotton trousers managed to make her visitor even more attractive than the brocade and lace of the night before.

'The moonlight didn't do you justice, Clemency Vaughan,' said Nick at last. 'You're tanned! I didn't think of you as a golden girl. Last night you were all silver and moonbeams. Today you're different.'

'So are you,' she said, then could have kicked herself as the smile vanished from his watchful face. 'I think I prefer you in everyday clothes, Mr Wood,' she added deliberately.

The single visible eye looked quizzical. 'Even without the mask?'

'Especially without the mask.'

He smiled again, and Clem relaxed.

'Perhaps we should introduce ourselves in the more usual way, if it's not a bit late in the day.' She held out her hand with mock formality. 'Good evening, Mr Wood. I'm so glad to meet you.'

'It's so kind of you to let me come.' Nick took her hand in his and held it tightly. 'Could it be fate that we live so near each other, Clemency?'

'It would have been more difficult if you'd been in Huddersfield, or Edinburgh, certainly, but not insurmountable.' She laughed breathlessly, her pulse accelerating at the touch of his hand. 'Won't you come into my parlour?'

'With pleasure!' He followed her into the sunlit room, limping slightly, she noticed with a pang. And in the bright light he looked even more haggard than the night before. His face was tanned to a brown much darker than her own, but it was thin and hollow-cheeked, with a smudge of fatigue below the one visible eye, which was a warm wine-brown, with a questioning look in the depths as he bore her scrutiny uneasily.

'They say the scar will never go completely,' he said at last.

'Do you mind?'

'Not for myself.'

'It makes no difference to me either,' she assured

him. 'I didn't know you without it, so for me you are as you are.'

'Warts and all?'

'Ah, but you're much handsomer than Oliver Cromwell.'

Nick laughed. 'Which wouldn't be difficult. While you must be bored with remarks about that beautiful face of yours.'

'Not bored, exactly. But so few people bother to find out there's more to me than just the way I look.'

'Which merely proves how unfair life can be.' He took possession of her hand again. 'Don't your women friends resent how generous Mother Nature's been to you, Clemency?'

'None that matter.' She felt mesmerised by the single, searching eye, burningly aware that for the past minute or two they had both been talking to disguise the current flowing between them like an electric charge that dried her mouth. She watched the skin grown taut over Nick's cheekbones and the small silence grew, and lengthened, and neither seemed able to look away, until at last Nick blinked, and swallowed hard.

'Where are they?' he asked.

She gazed at him blankly. 'Who?'

'The friends who live here with you.'

'Out,' she whispered.

Nick thrust a hand through his hair. 'Then we'd better get out of here. Now. Where—where would you like to eat?'

Clem ignored a persistent inner voice which counselled caution. 'I thought you might like to have supper here.' As she moved closer, she could see he was trembling, and raised a hand to touch his face, alarmed. 'Nick, are you ill?'

He shook his head, teeth clenched. 'No,' he said through them. 'Not ill.'

The trembling communicated itself to Clem; then, after only a moment's hesitation, she slid her arms round his waist and leaned her face against his chest, listening, shaken, to the thunder of his heartbeat. 'Tell me what's wrong,' she pleaded.

'Nothing's wrong,' he said in a tortured voice. 'In fact, nothing's ever felt so right before, but it may surprise you to know, Clemency Vaughan, that it's not my practice to fall on a girl within minutes of meeting her. On the other hand, if you don't move away right now my powers of self-control are in deep trouble.'

'Oh, is that all?' she said in relief, and held up her face. 'Then please kiss me, Nicholas Wood, because it's all I've been able to think about since last night.'

With a sound somewhere between a sigh and a groan, Nick did as she asked, wrapping his arms round her as his hungry mouth met hers. And this time, even without fantastic costumes and moonlit setting, the magic was even stronger than before. He pulled her to the couch and sat down with her on his lap, his lips both demanding and tender on hers, and Clem gave herself up to his embrace without reserve, exulting in the fire running through her veins. When neither could breathe, Nick took his mouth from hers, but only to kiss her nose, her eyes, her ears, until he returned to her parted, questing lips again, the tip of his tongue touching hers, then sliding deeper within to learn the contours of her mouth, as her arms slid round his neck to hold him closer. Time passed unnoticed, until at long last he raised his head and looked at her with a gleam in his undamaged eye.

'Have you any idea how much better I feel now?' he said huskily. 'I'm not sure I could have survived much longer without kissing you.'

'I know exactly how much, because I feel the same.' There seemed no point in hiding it. Clem smiled up at him sheepishly. 'I was so afraid you wouldn't ring, you know.'

'Are you mad, woman? I rang before you even got back here this morning!'

'I know, but until then I was sure you'd forget my number, or—or change your mind.'

He scowled blackly in disbelief. 'How could you think that? Don't you ever look in the mirror? Believe me, I wrote your number down the first opportunity I got, and woke up with it on the tip of my tongue.' He looked relaxed as he grinned down at her, very different now from the tense man of a few minutes before.

Clem's eyes gleamed, iridescent with pleasure. 'Did you really?'

'Of course I did.' He settled her more comfortably against his shoulder. 'I lay awake most of the night just wondering about you. How a ravishing creature like you could still be unattached. Unless you're not?' he added, scowling again into her glowing face.

'Of course I am—completely now. I bade Hugo a fond farewell over lunch today.'

'At lunch? Before you even heard from me?'

'Yes.'

He smoothed her hair back from her forehead, looking dazed. 'What would you have done if I hadn't rung back?'

'Nothing. What could I have done? You didn't give me *your* telephone number, and I had no idea where you lived, so that would have been that. But having met you I knew I couldn't marry Hugo anyway. Whether I ever saw you again or not.' Clem looked up at him very steadily. 'The moment you held me in your arms and kissed me, I realised I'd never really responded like that to a man in my entire life.'

'Not even Hugo?'

'No. So I let him down as lightly as possible.'

Nick rubbed his cheek against hers and gave a long, unsteady sigh. 'If I'm dreaming all this, I hope to God I never wake up.' He chuckled suddenly. 'Tomorrow I'm going to send the biggest bouquet of flowers she's ever had in her life to my aunt Evelyn.'

Clem looked up, smiling. 'Because she insisted you go to the ball?'

'Exactly.' He shook with sudden laughter. 'Perhaps you didn't realise, my darling, which of those characters last night happened to be my aunt. She was the plump lady in spangles with a wand—the Fairy Godmother herself!'

CHAPTER THREE

IT WAS so late before they even began to think of eating that Clem found she was starving as they faced each other across the table. Nevertheless they talked non-stop as they demolished Emma's chicken and worked their way through the bread and cheese and wine. In response to Nick's demands to know all about her, Clem described Robina Crichton's studio in Pimlico, where she helped create special-occasion clothes for her partner's well-connected friends and relatives, told him her evenings were spent at the cinema or the theatre, that she liked reading and walking in the park when it was fine. Nick was such an attentive, absorbed listener, she found it very easy to talk about her hopes and her ambitions, and found it necessary to apply mental brakes after a while, wary of going into too much detail. Yet. She was almost afraid of this blazing new awareness of the man encouraging her to reveal herself to him. It was all so new, yet at the same time so familiar. Her feeling of *déjà vu* was so strong, she almost believed they had known each other before in another life.

'Enough about me,' she said at last, as they sat over coffee. 'Tell me about you. What do you do?'

Nick took her hand in his as he stretched his legs

out cautiously. 'I'm a journalist—or was. I've been out of action for a while.'

Clem reached to touch gentle fingertips to his face. 'Because of this?'

He nodded. 'Didn't dodge quickly enough in Beirut. Got caught by a ricochet.'

'Your leg, too?'

His face went blank. 'You noticed the limp?'

'Yes. Like I noticed you've got a mole near your left ear, and your two front teeth are slightly crooked. Everything about you is important.'

He caught her in his arms. 'I can't believe this, Clemency Vaughan. My experience of women hasn't prepared me for someone as open and candid as you.'

She flushed. 'You think I should be more restrained,' she said flatly. 'Hide my feelings and try to be mysterious and so on.'

Nick's teeth gleamed white in his dark face as he looked down at her with unashamed possessiveness. 'No, don't. Artifice is unnecessary in your case, sweetheart.' He shook her gently. 'All the same, I need to keep reminding myself that less than twenty-four hours ago I didn't know you existed. Yet now——' He paused, his arms tightening, 'now, Clemency, I feel that all the time we've spent apart until last night has been irrelevant, wasted.'

Clem shivered and slid her arms round his neck, rubbing her smooth gold cheek against his unscarred one. 'That's exactly the point. Why waste time on silly pretence? I've never felt like this before about a man in my life, but of course, if it embarrasses you for me to say so——'

Nick silenced her by kissing her swiftly, holding her with exquisite tenderness, as though she were porcelain and might break if he were rough. It was a long time before he released her. 'The feeling I have at this moment can best be described as awe,' he said at last. 'I never expected to find a woman who could make me feel so deeply within minutes of meeting her. Especially now, when I look like something out of a horror film.'

Clem glared at him. 'Will you stop talking like that? I don't care if you're a dead ringer for the Hunchback of Notre-Dame! It's what's deep inside you that calls to something deep inside *me*, Nicholas Wood, nothing at all to do with the way you look, and I hope nothing to do with the way I look, either. And if I'm breaking all the rules by putting all my cards on the table far too soon I'm sorry, but that's the way it is.'

'Sorry?' He pulled her on to his lap, cradling her against his shoulder. 'Clemency—my darling, beautiful girl—how could I be sorry? It's just that I can't believe my luck.'

She looked up at him anxiously. 'If you were in Beirut, you must be a foreign correspondent. Does that mean you'll have to go abroad again soon?'

He shook his head. 'I'm officially on the sick list at the moment, but actually I'm working on a book I've been commissioned to write.'

Her eyes lit up with admiration. 'Really? What sort of book?'

He grinned. 'Intrigue, action, love on the run, with Afghanistan as a backdrop. Everything about it is clear in my mind from beginning to end, except the woman in the story. I just couldn't bring her to life, somehow, see her face clearly. Until now.'

She eyed him uneasily. 'You don't mean——'

'I do.' Suddenly he tipped her off his lap and took her by the hand to stand her in front of the mirror over the fireplace. 'Look,' he whispered. 'There she is.'

Clemency gazed at their reflections as he put an arm round her shoulders and stood with his cheek touching her hair.

'See,' he said softly. 'Beauty and——'

'Don't say it!' she said sharply, then smiled at him in the mirror. 'I think we look rather good together.'

Inwardly she was more than a little disturbed by the change in herself. At first glance her hair and face looked the same as usual, but a second look showed eyes which shone with a new brilliance, a brighter light which glowed from within. Even to herself, used to her own face in the mirror, her eyes shone back from her reflection like lamps. In contrast to her tan, she told herself, but knew this was nonsense. The reason for the radiance was holding her in his arms. It was the emotion Nicholas Wood evoked inside her which made her glow against his darkness, everything about her a

foil for his finely etched, bony good looks. His scar
and the eye-patch were mere tokens of emphasis,
adding to the charisma she'd responded to instinctively from the first moment he'd taken off the
mask.

'I look different,' she said, and turned to face
him. 'I *feel* so different, too; another person altogether from the Clemency Vaughan of this time
yesterday. Are you a magician, Nicholas Wood?
Because whatever spell I'm under has been cast by
you.'

His jaw clenched as he held her away from him,
and his gaze touched her like a caress as it roved
over her flushed face and bare tanned shoulders. 'If
you go on saying things like that, my darling, I
won't be responsible for the consequences. It can't
have escaped your notice that when you look at me
with that extraordinary light in your eyes I go to
pieces.' He looked at her hungrily. 'Will it shock
you if I confess I want you so badly this minute I
can't think straight?'

For answer Clem moved into his arms, offering
her mouth to him, and he pulled her against him
and kissed her savagely, his body vibrating with
need against hers.

'It's too sudden, too soon,' he muttered hoarsely
against her mouth, and she nodded blindly, her
fingers busy with the buttons of his shirt.

'I know, I know, but does it matter?' She slid her
hands over his bared chest.

'Clemency, for God's sake, I'm not sure I
can——'

'Then don't try.'

Two wide blue eyes stared up in luminous trust into the single dark one holding hers with such anguish, then Clem took her lover by the hand and led him up to the bedroom at the back of the house and closed the door behind them. It was dusk, but there was light enough for her to see the taut expression on his face, and she drew him to the bed and put a hand to his cheek, running gentle fingertips along the scar, tracing the outline of his mouth.

'Will you believe me if I tell you, Nicholas Wood, that I've slept alone in that bed for more years than I care to remember? That I've never in my life asked a man to make love to me. As I'm now asking *you*.'

Nick sat down on the bed abruptly, as if his legs had given out from under him. 'I felt I had to wait,' he said unsteadily. 'Try not to rush things——'

'Why?' She stood before him, her fingers untying the ribbons which secured her dress at the waist. 'I'm twenty-eight, Nick.' She slid out of the dress and tossed it aside on a chair. 'Time's a-wasting.'

Dark colour rushed into his face at the sight of her golden-skinned body in its frivolous scraps of satin, then the colour receded slowly, leaving the scar prominent against his skin. Almost reverently he drew her down to him, and stretched out on the bed as he held her against him with a great, shuddering sigh, as though he'd come home.

'I thought it would be enough for now just to hold you in my arms like this,' he said, against her quivering mouth, 'but it isn't. I want more, my lovely one, I want all of you. And I'd better make something very clear before I lose what little reason I have left.'

'What is it?'

'If I take you now, Clemency Vaughan, I shall expect to keep you. All to myself.'

She wriggled closer. 'I think that can be arranged.'

Nick drew away from her and stripped off his clothes, and what remained of hers. He ran worshipping fingers over her cheek, her throat, and downward until he held her breasts cupped in his hands, and he bent his head to put his mouth to each rose-red nipple in turn. She gasped and clutched him to her, and he slid his thigh between hers, plaiting their limbs together so that they cleaved closer and closer, open mouth to open mouth, tongue to tongue and breast to breast, angles and planes to curves and hollows until no part of one was separate from the other as at last, in natural progression, his body merged with hers in the way man has claimed woman ever since the Garden of Eden.

'There was something I didn't tell you, Nick,' Clem said quietly, long afterwards, when her powers of speech had returned.

Nick tensed in her arms. 'What is it?'

'When I told you I sleep in this bed alone, I meant it. I do. But for a time, years ago, I shared it with Evan.'

He lay very still for a moment or two, then turned on his side, taking her with him, settling her carefully against his shoulder, so that all she could see of him in the summer dusk was his sharp-carved profile, rendered blank by the black silk patch.

'And who was Evan?' he asked very softly.

'I met him in college. He was all set to be a graphic designer, and I was going to paint master-pieces.'

There was a pause.

'Where is he now?'

'He went climbing in the Cairngorms and fell to his death in a blizzard. We'd been living together for a year. He was twenty-one. So was I.'

'Tragic.' Nick's voice was carefully neutral. 'Did you love him, Clemency?'

She stared at the ceiling, trying to choose her words with care. 'We were loving friends, I suppose. He was lucky enough to get a good job straight away, and shared this house with a friend who moved north after a while, so Evan asked me to share instead, and it seemed like a good idea. My sister had just got married and I felt a bit lost, and Evan Rees was familiar, lively company; a bit wild and a lot of fun, but with the accent of home in his voice. So I—I shared his bed occasionally and washed his shirts and paid him a peppercorn rent out of my pittance for the magazine which took me on as dogsbody.'

'But did you *love* him?'

'I was fond of him, but only in the way I feel for Penry.' Clem felt the muscular body stiffen against hers.

'And who the hell is Penry?' he demanded.

'My brother; surgeon in embryo, at present registrar at St Ed's and constant threat to the chastity of the nursing staff therein.'

Nick chuckled, to her great relief, and drew her closer. 'How about Prince Charming of last night? God, was it only last night? Where did *he* come into your scheme of things?'

Clem thought about it before answering, then decided the truth was best, telling him Hugo had seemed the type of man it seemed sensible to marry. 'My sisters already have two children apiece, and I felt I needed to get a move on if ever I hoped to do the same.'

'Can't help feeling sorry for the poor blighter.'

'He'll soon find someone else.'

'But not like you.' He turned her towards him. 'There *is* no one like you. Unique's the word. The mould was broken after you were made, Clemency Vaughan.'

'Nick——' she began, but his mouth silenced her and his hands slid to her breasts, then her thighs, and the talking was over suddenly as the loving began again. And this time Nick was no longer subject to his own urgency, and could take time to tease and dawdle and play, until she twisted and turned beneath his clever hands and resorted quite shamelessly to ploys which made him quench the fire he'd started.

It was midnight when he left. Only the arrival of the taxi he ordered tore them apart at the door as he kissed her over and over again before he could bring himself to say goodnight. And when he was gone Clem forced herself to wash dishes and tidy up as though this were any other normal evening of her life. She was sitting on a stool in the kitchen, staring into space as coffee cooled in a mug in front of her, when Emma arrived home.

One look at Clem brought Emma rushing to throw her arms round her fiercely. 'Didn't the swine turn up after all?'

Clem's dazed eyes opened wide. 'Oh, yes. But he wouldn't stay.'

Emma moved back, frowning. 'You mean to say he came, had a drink, then said cheerio?'

'No, no. He left about twelve.'

'Twelve?'

'Yes. I meant he wouldn't stay the night.'

Emma sat down suddenly on another stool. 'Dear me, how unsporting of him.' She shook her head in wonder. 'Clem, in all the time I've lived here you've never let a man upstairs except to go to the bathroom. Yet you tell me you actually *asked* this one to stay the night, the very first time you spend an evening together?'

'Yes. Want some coffee?'

'Yes. Black and strong, please. I'm in shock.'

Clem laughed. 'What's so shocking? Hamish stays the night with you, sometimes. And Don does with Jane.'

Emma took pains to point out that both gentlemen in question enjoyed fiancé status, and had known their future brides some considerable time before being granted the privilege in question. 'It seems to me,' she finished, 'that this Nick of yours had no idea what a unique offer yours actually was.'

Clem put a steaming mug down in front of Emma. 'Yes, he does. I made it quite clear that I sleep alone in it when I showed him the bed.'

Emma choked on a mouthful of hot coffee. 'You—showed him the bed?'

'Yes. And made love with him in it. More than once, to be precise.' Clem's face lit with a luminous, dreaming smile. 'It was utterly perfect.'

Emma stared in dismay at the vision before her. 'Oh, Clem, for heaven's sake, be careful!'

'Too late for that. I'm in love at long last and I've no intention of being careful. I want the same as my sisters. And in Nick I've found it, I know.' The certainty in her voice did nothing at all to reassure the troubled Emma, who looked deeply shaken by Clem's statement. 'I rang Robina after Nick left, by the way,' added Clem casually.

'After midnight?'

'Robina's a night-bird. Anyway, I told her it was an emergency. I haven't had any time off for ages, with all the stuff for Ascot and the Heyford-Stuart wedding, so I asked if she could manage if I took next week off, as well as my holiday in Spain later on.'

'I see. And this Nick—doesn't he have to work at something?'

Clem told Emma about his accident and the book he was writing, then patted her friend's cheek, told her not to worry, and went off to bed to stare through the window at the same full moon she had watched the night before, reflected in the lake at Overbury Manor. It was hard to believe it was a mere twenty-four hours or so since Nicholas Wood had first materialised out of the darkness and turned her world upside-down. Or right side up, she thought, with a smile, as she stretched luxuriously in the bed where just a short time ago she'd experienced her first true taste of paradise.

Clem woke early next morning to the sight of Emma's face at the foot of the bed.

'Phone,' said Emma tersely, and went off to the bathroom.

Clem dived out of bed and ran downstairs to snatch up the receiver.

'Good morning, Highness,' said Nick's voice in her ear.

'Good morning.'

'I trust you slept well?'

'Like a log.'

'Sacrilege! How can such a ravishing creature describe herself as a log?'

'I sew better than I write.'

He laughed. 'My idea was to catch you before you took off to *start* sewing today. Could you come to my place tonight, darling? I'm sure your friends are great girls, but for now I want you all to myself. I was in no condition to think of practicalities last night when I left.'

Clem slid slowly down the wall until she sat cross-legged on the floor. 'All right. What time shall I come?'

'How early can you make it?'

'Not until about ten.'

'*Ten*? For God's sake, Clemency——'

'Ten this morning, if you like. I've taken some time off.'

Nick let out an explosive sigh. 'Witch! Make it nine.'

'No—too much traffic.'

'Take a taxi. I'll pay.'

'I'll be there about ten,' she insisted. 'I need time to make myself——'

'Not more beautiful. Please! A poor guy can only take so much.'

'I was going to say presentable. See you later.' Clem put the phone down, grinning at Emma, who stepped over her in disapproval on her way through the hall to the kitchen.

'I assume that was Nick. Coffee?'

'Yes, to both.' Clem leapt to her feet and put some bread in the toaster. 'Want some scrambled eggs?'

'No. I'm worried.'

'Over me? Don't be. I was bound to fall in love just once before I die, you know. And you can't say you ever cared much for Hugo.'

Emma sipped her coffee, looking depressed. 'True. I just wish you weren't so—so sudden about it all. What's this man got that all the others haven't had?'

'No idea. But whatever it is I want it—all of it. For keeps.'

Emma groaned, and prepared to depart for the

firm of Roehampton solicitors where both she and
Jane worked as legal secretaries. 'It's too late to say
be good, Clem. But just to please me, do try hard to
be careful.'

Clem waved her off, laughing, then sat down to a
large breakfast and the unusual pleasure of lingering over the morning paper before making herself
as beautiful as possible for the delectation of one
Nicholas Wood.

The taxi put her down later outside a large
Victorian house in a quiet street in Parson's Green.
A separate entrance led to the top-floor flat, which
was occupied by a smart young couple in advertis-
ing, but the main front door was Nick's sole pro-
perty, and gave access to the two lower storeys of
the house, which he occupied alone. As soon as
Clem rang the bell the door flew open and Nick
pulled her inside, kicking the door shut behind
them as he kissed her for some considerable time
before letting her say a word.

'Unbelievable,' he said when he let her go. He
looked her up and down, and shook his head.
'When I'm away from you I'm positive my memory
exaggerates. Then the moment I lay eyes on you
again I realise it hasn't even done you justice.'

'It's only window-dressing, Nick.' Clem
examined him in turn. He looked bright and
refreshed this morning, in a pale blue shirt and
faded jeans which hugged his narrow hips. 'You
look better today. Less haggard.'

'I've been given some quite miraculous therapy.'
He raised an eyebrow as bright colour flooded from

the neckline of her white shirt to the roots of her hair, and he shook his head, marvelling. 'Oh, Clemency, Clemency, you are something!'

She lifted her chin and stalked past him, demanding to see his part of the house, which was furnished for comfort rather than style, with lots of leather, and thin Eastern carpets, and books and records in such profusion that they dominated the entire living area.

'I sleep up there,' he said, jerking his head towards the stairs. 'I don't suppose you'd care to inspect?' He grinned as she shook her head primly. 'I wasn't suggesting we go to bed, darling.'

'Weren't you?' she challenged.

Nick's face took on a look that made her pulse race. 'I suppose I was, subconsciously,' he said slowly. 'To be brutally honest, I haven't been able to think of anything else since I left you last night. I still can't believe my luck in having you here with me right now. I lay awake last night trying to think of ways to get through the day until I could be with you again tonight, then, miracle of miracles, you're here. And God help me, I still can't think of anything else.'

Clem digested this in silence. 'I feel the same,' she said at last, smiling at him rather shakily. 'Though I'm certain I shouldn't admit it. But I don't think we should make love again until we've spent several hours doing other things. Ordinary things. We've started our story sort of in the middle, Nick. I feel we need to back-pedal a bit. Start at the beginning. Find out what else makes each other tick, besides the—the other thing.'

He nodded gravely, and reached out a hand to touch her cheek. 'Whatever you want. Now and always.'

Clemency's heart leapt at the 'always', and to hide it she went out with him to explore the small garden behind the house.

'It's too lovely a day to waste indoors, Nick. Let's have a picnic lunch out here, and sunbathe. I love the sun, and hardly ever have much chance to enjoy it. By the time I'm free at the weekend it's raining, more often than not.'

Nick applauded the suggestion, and dragged old deckchairs from a garden shed, and even a rusty old table they could use for their picnic. Afterwards they went shopping, and bought ham carved from the bone, great batons of crusty bread, lots of salad greens and fruit and several bottles of wine.

'Enough for a siege!' gasped Clemency as they reached the house.

'The idea of a siege sounds good—if it's just you and me holed up together.' He grinned as he opened the wine, then popped an expensive early strawberry between her lips as she washed lettuce. 'You know, Miss Vaughan, this is all a lot of fun. I like playing house with you.'

'Good. Peel those eggs, then. They should be done by now.'

Clem was in agreement with Nick. It *was* fun to eat out in the small garden with its moss-spattered patch of lawn. The houses around them were empty during the day, anyway, he told her, so she could sunbathe to her heart's content, secure from all eyes but his.

'Or eye!' he corrected solemnly.

She giggled. 'You sound like the little yellow god. Good thing your eye's not green.'

He regarded her contemplatively. 'It could be, if you make me jealous. I've never thought of myself as the jealous type before, but I rather fancy it might be different in your case.'

'You won't be put to the test, because I don't believe in playing silly games,' she assured him with energy.

They lay back in the old striped chairs, holding hands until it was too hot for comfort in their windless little retreat, and then went indoors to sit with long, cool drinks at hand while Clem demanded details of the places Nick had been and eye-witness accounts of all the exciting incidents in his career. He told her things which made her eyes open in astonishment, then soften with tears as he described his experiences from the time when he had started as a very green reporter in Cambodia, progressing to various other troubled parts of the globe, mainly in Africa and the Gulf of Hormuz.

'I wanted to go to the Falklands, but that didn't come off,' he said with regret.

Clem blenched at the mere idea of the danger he had obviously been exposed to, and eyed him questioningly across her glass. 'And now? Will you stay in this country from now on?'

'I might. It depends.'

'On what?'

'The incentives I get to stay here.'

'The book, you mean.'

Nick regarded her very intently. 'That, and other things.' He smiled. 'Now, what would you like to do this evening?'

Clem didn't mind what they did, as long as they did it together, and Nick took her out for a meal to a small Italian restaurant in the Fulham Road, a place where Nick was obviously well-known, since the proprietor came to the table to be introduced and brought his wife to meet Nick's 'lovely lady'. Afterwards Nick held her hand as they walked back through the hot summer streets, and when they reached the house Clem went to the telephone and rang Emma to say she was staying the night with Nick.

She put the phone down and turned to see Nick standing watching her, with a strange look on his tense face.

'You did want me to?' she said uncertainly, and he dived across the space between them, his mouth hungry on hers as he pulled her into his arms.

'Of course I want you to stay,' he muttered raggedly between kisses. 'I didn't know how the hell to ask!'

She laughed joyously and threaded her fingers through his untidy dark hair, her eyes alight with the warmth mounting inside her. 'I suppose I should have waited until I *was* asked!'

For answer Nick ran with her upstairs to his bedroom, which was large and shadowy, with windows he opened wide to the warm night. They

stood together, arms round each other as they
looked up at the familiar moon, and Clem shivered a
little. He drew her down to sit on the bed, then went
on his knees in front of her. He slid his arms round
her waist and looked deep into her eyes, then kissed
them shut and put his good cheek against hers,
holding her with such tenderness she trembled.

'I never knew there was anyone in the world like
you, my darling,' he whispered.

'Nick——'

'No, let me say my piece. I've been all over the
world—hell-holes, beautiful places, I've lost count of
them. But never, anywhere, have I laid eyes on
anyone to compare with you.'

Clem shook her head, trying to break free. 'But
Nick, please listen, there's something you should
know——'

'I know *you* already. And if you're harbouring
any dark secrets, they're in the past.' He turned her
face up to his, suddenly rough. 'Unless there's
some other man I should know about in the
present?'

'There's no other man, Nick, I swear, but——'

'Then what else is there to know? Just kiss me,
for God's sake. I've been good as gold all day and I
want my reward.'

And helplessly Clem obeyed, forgetting everything as his lips met hers. By the time she was
naked in his arms, nothing in the world mattered
but the touch of his fingers playing harmonies on
her skin and the feel of his mouth as it paid homage
to every last inch of her, from her sunburned toes

to the crown of her head.

And this time some of the initial diffidence had gone. They knew each other better now. Each had learned a little of what pleased the other, and took infinite pleasure in learning more. Soon Clem was fierce with need, and Nick fierce in his pride at assuaging it, until at last the storm was over and they were quiet in each other's arms, awestruck by the force of feeling each unleashed in the other.

They waited until the evening of the next day before going round to the house in Putney to collect some clothes for Clem, who made no bones about wanting to show Nick off to Emma and Jane.

'Show me off?' he said, scowling, and she laughed and kissed him.

'Yes. Because I want them to meet the man I—I met at the ball,' she said, and flushed as his eye fixed her with a bright, questioning look.

I must be mad, thought Clem wildly. She had almost said 'the man I love', and Nick looked dazed as though he suspected as much, but couldn't believe it. Neither could Clem. After a mere three days it seemed rash in the extreme to assume she actually loved this haggard stranger; that Nicholas Wood was all she'd ever dreamed of and would ever want, world without end. Yet it looked perilously like the truth. And Clem could tell Emma and Jane were in very little doubt about her feelings, either, when they were confronted with Nicholas Wood in person for the first time that night.

'So you're the famous Beast,' said Emma with characteristic bluntness. 'Haven't we met somewhere? You look familiar.'

'My God,' remonstrated Jane, 'that line went out with the Ark! Hello, Nicholas, I'm Jane Taylor, and pay no attention to my frank friend here. Em's famous for her sledgehammer approach.'

Nick laughed as he was directed to the most comfortable chair in the room, while both girls plied him with offers of coffee, brandy, food, cigarettes. 'Yes to the first, and no, thanks, to the rest. Clemency cooked a meal for me before we came.'

Clem flushed to the roots of her hair as her friends turned speculative eyes on her, and escaped upstairs to collect some clothes while the girls fussed over Nick. She was zipping a holdall when Emma joined her a few minutes later.

'Do you like him, Emma?' she said expectantly.

'Yes, I do. And I can certainly understand why.'

'Why what?'

Emma sat down on the bed, looking very serious. 'Why you've gone completely off your trolley about him.'

'Am I so transparent, then?'

'So much so, it's frightening, Clem.'

'Stop worrying!' Clem patted Emma's shoulder. 'I'm a big girl, love. By no means straight out of the egg.'

'That's what *is* worrying. You were stunning enough to look at before, God knows, but now——' Emma spread her hands. 'It dazzles me to look at you.'

Clem laughed, and gave a careless glance in the mirror. 'Nonsense! It's the same old me, I promise.

By the way, I'm staying for a couple of days at Nick's, then we're going down to Llanhowell for the weekend.'

Emma's eyebrows rose. 'Last weekend Hugo, this weekend Nick. Won't your parents be confused?'

'Not once they've met Nick.' Clem checked on her belongings. 'Right, let's go, before Jane gets too comfortable down there with my man.'

'Is that what he is?'

'I think so.' Clem's blue eyes shone with certainty as they met Emma's. 'In fact, I know he is. Would it sound too saccharine for words to say I recognised him from the first? The minute Nick pulled that incredible mask off, I knew I'd found the man I'd been looking for all my life.'

'Oh dear, oh dear. I just hope it won't end in tears, that's all,' said Emma, unappeased.

Clem laughed and gave her friend a hug, then ran downstairs, handing her bag to Nick as he met her in the hall. He slid his free arm round her waist and smiled at Emma and Jane.

'I enjoyed meeting you both. See you again soon.'

It was patently obvious to both girls that neither the tall, dark man nor their glowing, radiant friend could wait to be alone together again, and Jane exchanged a wry look with Emma, then opened the front door.

'Off you go, then, children. Be good.'

Nick looked very deliberately at each girl in turn and smiled in reassurance. 'I'll take great care of her, I promise.'

Emma eyed him steadily. 'Do that, Nicholas Wood. We're quite fond of her, you know.'

Clem flushed, but Nick nodded, unruffled. 'Don't worry. So am I.'

When they were in a taxi on their way back to Parson's Green, Clem smiled ruefully at him. 'I hope Emma didn't embarrass you.'

He grinned down at her, sliding an arm round her waist. 'It would take more than Miss Emma Reeves to do that, darling. Besides, after some of the things I've seen in various places round the globe, concern for other human beings is something I appreciate in anyone, believe me. Your friends' concern for you is highly laudable, but unnecessary, you know. I meant what I said.'

Clem stayed silent after that, mulling over his words. It seemed Nick was telling her he was fond of her. Which was all right in its way, of course. But not enough. Not nearly enough. She wanted him head over heels in love with her, as she was with him. To be consumed with this desperate longing to be as close as humanly possible, physically and mentally, to be together for the rest of their lives. In short, marriage; a state she had never yearned for before with any man until now. It was true she had contemplated it with Hugo, at the dictate of her brain, but had never longed for it with all her heart as she did now with Nick. After only a few days spent in his company she knew beyond any shadow of doubt that he was the only man capable of providing the happy ending to her own particular story.

'Penny for them,' said Nick, as the taxi drew up outside the house.

Clem shook her head, smiling. 'Not for sale.'

She put thoughts of marriage firmly from her head, determined to enjoy whatever life offered, refusing to allow doubts about the future to cloud the present, which passed in a dreamlike sequence of laughing and loving, and the sheer enjoyment of being together as she wandered with Nick along the Fulham Road, windowgazing at antiques and pictures, or patronising the various fashionable little eating places in the neighbourhood. They frequented the White Horse at lunchtime in Parson's Green, where Nick cracked jokes with a cheerful young Australian barman, then afterwards they wandered in Fulham Palace Gardens, enjoying the afternoon sun, pretending they were walking in the country in the cottage-garden atmosphere of its seclusion. They bought luscious pastries to eat with the tea they drank on the tiny patch of lawn behind Nick's house, and later when it was cooler they prepared a meal together, or went out to eat, and one evening went to the cinema near Putney Bridge, squabbling amicably over their choice of the three films on offer, and afterwards sitting hand in hand in the darkness, the choice of film irrelevant, since their enjoyment was heightened by the simple fact of watching it in each other's company.

CHAPTER FOUR

THE WEEKEND brought Clem back to earth before she was ready for it. The outer world intruded on her idyll in the shape of Nick's agent, who rang him on the Thursday evening with a reminder of lunch with his editor the following day.

'Blast!' Nick scowled as he rummaged for the diary on his desk. 'I'd forgotten.' He looked across at Clem, who lay full length on the leather chesterfield across the room, watching him. 'Do you realise you've made me forget anything existed other than you and me? While all the time there's a noisy, brash world out there ready to pounce on a poor be-glamoured mortal and haul him kicking and screaming back to reality.'

Clem sighed. 'Does this mean you can't make it this weekend?'

'No, of course not. But I can't get there as early as planned, obviously. Must you start off in the morning?'

'It's my father's birthday. I promised Mother I'd be there early to help with dinner.' Clem sat up, stretching. 'You'll just have to follow on later, after this lunch of yours.'

'Not much option, I suppose.' Nick eyed her morosely. 'If you refuse to wait for me at least make sure you provide me with detailed instructions, so I can roll up in good time to wish your father many happy returns.'

'Are you sure you're up to driving all that way?' She smiled at him coaxingly. 'Take the train, Nick—please. I could meet you with Dad's car in Newport.'

He shook his head and let himself down beside her. 'No, I'll be fine, I promise. On my own in the car I can wear dark glasses instead of the patch, which takes care of the vision—and there's nothing wrong with my leg now——'

'True,' she murmured, and ran a delicately questing finger along his thigh.

Nick breathed in sharply and captured her hand. 'So I'll drive down the M4, cross the Severn Bridge, and I'll be in Llanhowell if not afore ye, at least in time for dinner.'

Clem chuckled at his pronounciation. 'Not *Clan*howell, Englishman. *Ll*anhowell. Put a little breath in before the L.'

'I can't reproduce the exact lilt. Yours is unique.'

'Not a bit of it. We Vaughans all talk alike.'

'Impossible.' He moved nearer, drawing her against him. 'There couldn't be anyone like you in the whole wide world, Highness.' He laid a finger on lips that opened to protest. 'No, don't let's talk any more right now. Let's just do this, and this . . .' He laid his mouth on hers and pushed her back on the couch and began to caress her in a way that promptly drove thoughts of anything but his love-making from her head. They caught fire from each other's urgency. Clem pulled Nick's shirt free from his jeans and ran her fingers up his spine, putting her open mouth against his shoulder, breathing in the warm, clean scent of his heated skin, delighted as his muscles tensed beneath her wandering fingers. Soon he could bear it no longer and sprang to his feet, taking her by the hand, pulling her along with him as he strode upstairs to the cool bedroom. They were both breathing raggedly as he undressed her in the half-dark and laid her urgently on the bed, taking her with no preliminaries of any kind, their mutual need so intense that nothing was necessary to their pleasure beyond the meeting of two bodies already so well-tuned to each other that they reached crescendo swiftly in perfect harmony, and lay locked together in wonder afterwards, as always, at the perfection of their union.

'I'm sorry,' murmured Nick at last. 'I was intemperate.'

'I liked it like that.'

'As though I'd die if I didn't have you?'

'Is that how you felt?'

'Yes.'

Clem stretched, luxuriating in the feel of his hard body against hers. She stroked his hair, her fingers halting as they encountered the cord of the eye-patch he stubbornly refused to take off. 'Let me see your eye, Nick.'

He rolled away on to his back and stared at the ceiling. 'No.'

'Why not?'

'It's ugly.'

'What difference does that make?'

'A lot. To me, anyway.'

Clem lay in silence, achingly conscious of his tension. 'I've seen the scar on your leg,' she pointed out after a time.

'That's different.'

She was sure that whatever lay under the patch would be a lot less disturbing than the picture her imagination kept conjuring up, but she gave in at once. 'All right, Nick, I won't nag any more.'

He turned towards her and pulled her close, rubbing his good cheek against hers. 'Everyone needs to keep something back, Clemency.' He stared down at her. 'I'm sure there are plenty of things about you I don't know, even though we've talked non-stop about ourselves for days, but I honestly believe every individual must hang on to something of themselves—just to remain an individual.'

Clem wasn't sure she liked the sound of that. 'You mean I've been too forthcoming about the way I feel for you?'

'God almighty, no!' He shook her hard. 'That's not what I meant at all. I delight in your honesty and your lack of affectation. Your response to me has done more for my convalescence than anything the medical profession could ever have come up with, apart from actual surgery.'

Clem detached herself gently and wrapped herself in his cotton dressing-gown, then went over to one of the windows to look down at the moonlit garden. Nick lay very still, watching her, his face obscured by shadow.

'You mean that between us you would always expect areas of our lives to remain closed books to each other?' she asked.

'Not exactly.' He locked his hands behind his head. 'I meant that no human being should ever demand everything of another.'

Clem thought this over at length, sorry now she had asked to see his eye. Yet the black silk patch still represented a barrier between them in some strange way. While whatever lay beneath it remained hidden from her she had the illogical feeling Nick could never wholly be hers. She jumped as his arms slid round her waist from behind.

'You gave me a fright!' she said, breathless.

'Did I? One learns to move quietly when necessary in my line of business.'

'Very likely. But I don't appreciate being crept up on.'

He smoothed the hair away from the nape of her neck, opening his mouth against her skin, so that she felt his lips and tongue, warm and persuasive, as they roved, planting kisses in the hollows behind her ears, raising trickles of response along her spine. He turned her in his arms and kissed her. 'If it means so much,' he muttered against her mouth, 'I'll take off the patch, since it's only moonlight. I'm not up to the full light of day yet. But promise not to scream.'

She held her breath as his hands went to the cord that secured the patch, nervous now that, Pandora-like, she had her wish, as Nick turned away to toss the patch on the dressing-table, then back again so that moonlight shone fully on his face. Relief flooded her as she looked steadily at the scar which puckered his eyelid and held it half open, then furrowed deeply through his heavy eyebrow before continuing up into his hair on the path already familiar to her. Instinctively she moved to touch a hand to his cheek, then stretched up to kiss the corner of the maltreated eye.

'So that's all it is,' she said scornfully, as he replaced the patch.

'Isn't it enough?' he demanded.

'More than enough, when I think of the pain you must have suffered—how easily you could have been killed. But nothing at all in terms of revulsion, on my part or anyone else's! Has everything been done that can be done?'

'Not yet. The vision's impaired in the eye itself, of course, but plastic surgery will improve my appearance soon. And until I can close my eye fully I'm advised to wear the patch.' Nick held her lightly. 'Can you put up with it until I've been re-modelled?'

'Now I can.' Her chin lifted. 'Because I know. Not that there could have been anything under that patch that would have made a scrap of difference. And,' she added tartly, 'it's the only secret I'll ever ask about, I promise.'

His face was inscrutable. 'So you won't be angry if you happen to discover other things I didn't mention?'

'No.' Her eyes narrowed. 'Unless, of course, you're about to tell me you're a married man,

Nicholas Wood.'

'No. I've had relationships of varying importance in the past—I won't deny that. But I've never found anyone I wanted to marry. Until now.'

Clem stood very still, her lashes falling to hide her eyes. Until now. The blood throbbed in her veins, she could hear the traffic outside, music from someone's radio through the open window, but she felt like one of the posies favoured by the Victorians, enclosed in glass in a cloche of silence.

'Clemency,' Nick whispered, and drew her unresisting body against his. He smoothed the dressing-gown away, then bent and picked her up, carrying her to the bed. He laid her down in a shaft of moonlight which turned her golden skin to marble, and he hung over her in silence, as if the sight of her lying there inspired reverence rather than urgency and heat.

Clem held up her arms in mute invitation and he sank down into them, stretching himself beside her as he held her close with a tenderness that thickened her throat with tears that reached her eyes and overflowed until he tasted their salt on his lips.

'Darling, don't cry!'

'I rarely do,' she whispered, sniffing, and he took her face in his hands and kissed the thick, damp lashes and wet cheeks, licking the tears away with a tongue that quickly grew bolder, flicking over the contours of her lips, then thrusting boldly between them as her quivering mouth opened eagerly. Suddenly Clem was no longer still. As Nick's mouth grew more urgent her hips thrust upwards, and he laughed deep in his throat and slid his hands down to her breasts, which rose to his touch, taut under his stroking fingers, the nipples hard as he teased them with bold lips and delicately grazing teeth, before moving his mouth lower, to her waist, her navel, and on down to the silky curls below, to invade their privacy and discover the exact nature of her response to his caresses.

'Please!' she gasped, and he poised over her, dark and tense with a desire that matched her own in the final moment before he gave in to her pleas and began to make love to her with all the subtlety at his command, until at last his control snapped and they moved together convulsively, in a basic need that joined them in the few throbbing, fleeting moments of unity nature allows.

'Happy Birthday, Dad!'

Dr Harry Vaughan smiled warmly at the radiant apparition advancing towards him outside Newport station the following afternoon, and hugged his daughter fondly. 'You look well, sweetheart! A different girl from last weekend. Your mother was a bit worried.'

Clem settled herself in the car with a contented sigh as her father threaded through the busy Friday traffic and headed out of Newport on the Maindee road.

'Was Mother surprised I invited someone else this weekend, Dad?'

Dr Vaughan grinned. 'Curious, rather. So am I.

How come we got Hugo Barrington last week, and
some chap we've never heard of this week?'

Clem explained at length, her happiness
radiating from her as she talked non-stop about
Nicholas Wood all the way to the Cauldra
roundabout, and long after they'd turned off on the
dual carriageway to Monmouth. Dr Vaughan was,
fortunately for his patients, an attentive listener,
and he let his daughter pour out her excitement
over the new man in her life without interruption
until she ran out of steam.

'Does this mean,' he said, when his daughter
paused for breath, 'that at the ripe old age of
twenty-eight you've finally fallen in love?'

Clem nodded, her eyes shining as she smiled up
at her father. 'Yes. At long last I know what Kit
and Chatty meant, about recognising the right man
when I found him.' She shook her head. 'I
genuinely thought I'd never find someone
who—who makes me feel the way I do for Nick.'

'Neither did your mother. She'll be pleased.'

'Are you?'

He slanted a whimsical smile at his daughter's
anxious face. 'Let's say I look forward to meeting
this Nicholas Wood. Very much.'

Angharad Vaughan took one look at the glowing
daughter who burst into the kitchen, and needed no
further enlightenment. She had seen that particular
radiance before, on the faces of her other two
daughters, had personal experience herself of the
feeling that generated it, when she first met a
medical student by the name of Harry Vaughan.

Clem's excited spate of explanations merely served as confirmation that Mrs Vaughan's one remaining single daughter hoped to change her status as soon as this extraordinary wonderful man called Nicholas Wood officially popped the question.

All through the afternoon Clem worked with her mother on the birthday dinner, tireless in her joyous anticipation of Nick's imminent arrival, the mere prospect of which lent enchantment to even mundane tasks like scrubbing new potatoes and polishing knives and forks.

It would be just the four of them, explained Mrs Vaughan, after her husband had left for his afternoon surgery. Kit and Reid were still coping with the aftermath of their sons' German measles, and of course it was high season at the hotel Charity's husband Luiz owned near Gerona in Spain.

'How about Penry?' asked Clem.

'On duty this weekend, unfortunately. He dashed down yesterday instead and went off to the local with his father as a sort of substitute celebration—men only.' Mrs Vaughan smiled. 'An arrangement I deeply appreciated. After feeding my son, I was only too pleased to put my feet up on my own before tackling tonight's menu.'

Clem giggled. 'The walking appetite! How that boy eats!'

'That "boy", as you put it, is only a year or so younger than you, Grandma! How old is this Nicholas of yours, by the way?'

'No idea. Thirty something, I suppose. I haven't asked.'

Mrs Vaughan asked a few questions about Nick's family and background, and laughed when Clem proved vague on hard facts. 'What *have* you been talking about all week, child?'

'Ourselves.' Clem's brilliant blue eyes softened to dreaminess. 'Funny, isn't it. This time last week I had no idea Nick even existed. And now I can't imagine life without him.'

Mrs Vaughan's eyebrows rose. 'It hasn't taken you long to decide that.'

Clem met her mother's questioning look point blank. 'I knew it from almost the first moment I set eyes on him.'

'Just like Charity did with Luiz, I suppose.'

'Only I'm ten years behind!'

Mrs Vaughan laughed. 'Go and change. If my memory serves me correctly, being in love adds considerably to the time necessary for prettying up, if Kit and Charity were anything to go by. You've only got an hour before your Nicholas is due, so get moving.'

The doorbell rang slightly less than an hour later, just as Clem was putting the finishing touches to her face, and Dr Vaughan was relaxing over a much-needed gin and tonic with his wife in the sitting-room. Clem raced downstairs, shouting, "I'll answer it," and threw open the front door expectantly, her face blank with amazement as she found, instead of the lean brown person of Nicholas Wood, an even darker-skinned man, elegant in a lightweight fawn suit, grey eyes gleaming in greeting under light brown hair, and in the crook of his arm a tall, voluptuously curved beauty with a mass of curling ash-fair hair, her cornflower-blue eyes alight with mischievous laughter in a face identical to the one Clemency Vaughan saw in her own mirror every morning.

'Surprise, Clem!' cried Charity, and held out her arms to her twin, who fell into them, hugging her and crowing with laughter as Luiz Santana detached his sister-in-law from his wife's arms and demanded, and received, his own kiss in greeting.

'*Gran Dios*,' he breathed in wonder, as he held Clem at arm's length. 'All the time I forget how much you two are alike, until I see you together again.'

'Never mind that.' Chatty pulled her sister back. 'Don't let's go in yet.' She eyed Clem's face closely. 'So who is he, then?'

'Who's who?'

'The man who's switched your light on, baby sister.'

Clem needed no urging to embark on her tale yet again, or as much of it as she needed to tell. From the time they could first speak the twins had possessed their own particular form of verbal shorthand, and Chatty would need only the bare bones of the story to know the whole, as always.

Their parents came hurrying from the house, smiling in delight at the unexpected arrivals, hardly able to believe their eyes. Luiz explained that his darling daughters had been entrusted to the care of his cousin Milagrita and her husband Juan Carreras in Granada, for the short time required.

'They will spoil the *ninas*, of course,' he laughed, 'but it is only a short time, because I cannot afford to be away from the hotel for longer than a day or so at this time of the year.'

'Luiz's uncle nobly volunteered to keep an eye on the place until we get back, otherwise we'd never have managed it.' Charity kissed her father affectionately. 'Couldn't pass up the chance to wish my dear old Dad many happy returns, now, could I?'

In all the excitement Clem had forgotten the time. But when her mother retreated to the kitchen to check on the meal she realised it was late. She frowned, then shrugged, smiling, as Charity raised an eyebrow.

'Nick's a bit later than expected. Usual Friday traffic, I expect.'

But an hour after that, when dinner could wait no longer, and as many drinks had been consumed as was prudent, Clem was very worried indeed.

'I'll give Nick's house a ring, just in case——' She left the rest of her thought unspoken, and stood in the hall, tense with anxiety, as she listened to Nick's unanswered phone ringing.

'He must be somewhere en route,' she said cheerfully, as she joined the others, and avoiding Charity's all-seeing eye. Determined not to spoil her father's birthday celebration, Clem talked vivaciously, catching up on news of her nieces, Dolly and Luiza, offering congratulations on the forthcoming event as, at her own insistence, they all went in to dinner.

'A son this time, I suppose,' she said, grinning,

and Luiz Santana laid a hand caressingly on his wife's arm.

'It is of no importance, a son or a daughter, only that my wife is safe and the child healthy.' The look on his face as he gazed down at Charity gave Clem a sharp pang, underlining the fact that Nick was missing.

All evening, as the minutes ticked by, Clem gave the greatest performance of her life as she battled hard not to ruin the occasion for everyone else. But as she laughed and talked her mind was frantic with worry, as she imagined Nick in a car crash, injured or—no, she told herself firmly. He couldn't be dead. She would know. But what in heaven's name had happened to him? Why hadn't he rung? Eventually she excused herself from the others and went into her father's study to try Nick's number one last time before she went to bed. Her heart turned over as this time Nick's deep voice barked in answer.

'Nick, it's Clemency. For God's sake, what happened? Are you all right, darling?'

'Yes,' he interrupted stonily. 'Or perhaps I should say as well as can be expected.'

'Did something go wrong at the lunch? I've been out of my mind all night, Nick——'

'And I've been out of mine all week. But not any longer. In fact you could say I'm in my right mind at last. So let's just call it quits, my dear. It was great fun and all that, but obviously just one of those things, as the song says.'

Clem's knees gave, and she sat down abruptly on the edge of her father's desk. Every drop of blood in her veins seemed to turn into ice, as she stared blindly through the window, wondering if this were a nightmare; if she were likely to wake up any minute to find the last week had all been a dream.

'What exactly are you saying?' she asked carefully.

Nick laughed, a sound that chilled her to the bone. 'It's over. Finished. Kaput. You're a bright girl, Clemency, you know very well what I'm saying.'

Clem knew, but she just couldn't take it in. This was the man who'd kissed her goodbye this morning with such tenderness, such—such *love*. How could he be saying it was all over between them? Perhaps she hadn't heard him properly. 'Are you saying that you don't want me any more, Nick?'

'No,' he said savagely. 'I still *want* you, God help me. But I'll get over that in time, never fear. There are other women in the world. But as far as you and I are concerned, that's it. In short, from now on just stay out of my life.'

He hung up, and after a long, long time Clem replaced the receiver and walked slowly towards the door. It opened before she reached it, and Charity stood in her path, staring at her in horror.

'Oh, my God. Clem—love!' She threw her arms round Clem and held her tight, and a little of the numbness went, and Clem's teeth began to chatter, great tremors running through her body as Charity kept up a non-stop flow of soothing encouragement as she drew her gently towards the stairs. Clem realised vaguely that her knees were buckling. Her legs refused to hold her up.

'S-sorry,' she got out with difficulty. 'Feel—funny.'

'Luiz! Dad!' yelled Charity, and her husband came down the stairs three at a time, converging with the Vaughans as they ran into the hall from the sitting-room.

'*Dios!*' Following his father-in-law's swift instructions, Luiz carried the shivering girl upstairs, while Dr Vaughan ran for his bag before hurrying after the others to the room Clem and Charity had shared as children.

'She's in shock,' said Dr Vaughan tersely. 'What the hell's happened?'

'Never mind now,' said his wife, white-faced, and hurried off to fill a hot-water bottle while Charity held her sister in her arms on the bed.

Dr Vaughan gave his daughter a swift examination, checked the racing pulse, then produced a capsule from his bag. 'Water,' he commanded, and Luiz ran to fill a toothmug at the washbasin. Without ceremony Charity prized apart the chattering teeth and popped the capsule in Clem's mouth, then held the glass for her to drink, water spilling over them both before her object was achieved.

'All right, Dad, I'll see to her.' Charity turned to smile in reassurance as Angharad Vaughan appeared. 'She'll be fine in a while, Mother. Better to leave her with me.'

Mrs Vaughan looked as shattered as Clem, but she nodded briskly. 'Yes, darling, I know. But call the instant you need anything.'

After the reluctant departure of the Vaughans, Luiz Santana scowled blackly as he smoothed his wife's hair.

'I would give much to kill this—this Nicholas Wood.'

Charity nodded grimly. 'I'd help.'

'I'm—not—dead,' said Clem faintly. 'No need to—hold a wake.'

'What happened?' demanded Charity. 'Did you speak to him? What did the brute *say* to you?'

Clem's eyes focused with difficulty on the two anxious faces hanging over her. 'Not a lot. Just—to stay out of his life.'

Luiz swore sibilantly in his native tongue, his eyes bright with rage.

Charity gripped Clem's hand fiercely. 'Did he give a reason?'

'No.' Clem experimented with unruly lips and found she could manage a faint smile, now her teeth had quietened down. 'Today was our first time apart since—since we got together. I suppose he had time to think. Time to reconsider. I don't know.' Her eyelids drooped. 'What's Dad given me? My tongue feels numb.'

'A mild sedative.'

'Sorry I fell apart. Never felt quite like that before. I thought I was dying.' Her eyes opened on Charity's. 'I think a bit of me *did*, Chatty.'

Charity swallowed hard, then held up her face for her husband's kiss. 'Go to bed, *mi amor*. I'll join you as soon as Clem's settled.'

Luiz kissed the beautiful, upturned mouth, then bent to touch his lips to Clem's cold cheek. '*Buenas noches, chica.* Do not grieve. There are other men. Come to us in Cabo Feliz soon. Play with the children and lie in the sun—and forget.'

Clem smiled drowsily. 'Thank you, Luiz.'

Charity went to the door with her husband for another kiss, then undressed her sister and sponged her face. 'Did you sleep with this man?' she asked bluntly.

'Not a lot. We made love most of the time.'

Charity groaned. 'Oh, Clem! I'm so sorry, love. Have a good cry, for pity's sake!'

'No tears,' muttered Clem indistinctly. 'Can't cry without tears.'

'I just wish there was something I could do!'

Clem's eyes opened wide for a moment. 'No one can do a thing, Chatty. Except Nick. And he doesn't want me any more.' Her lids closed over the forlorn lost look, and she gave herself up to blessed oblivion as Charity tiptoed away, the tears her twin should have been shedding streaming down her own face as she fled to the comfort of her husband's arms.

CHAPTER FIVE

LADY ROBINA CRICHTON was the daughter of an earl, wife to the son of another, and indulged her considerable artistic and business flair by designing and making grand-occasion dresses for favoured friends in her own social circle. Clem and Charity had first come across her in art college, but it was only after Evan Rees died that Clem ran into her again. Robina, tall and commanding, with chestnut hair and fair, flawless skin, had spotted Clem quite by chance through the window of a coffee bar one day, and had sailed into the small, crowded café, superbly indifferent to curious looks as she hailed Clem with delight. She promptly ordered fresh coffee and settled herself to catch up on what had happened to them both since college, eager to tell Clem about her new venture. She described it as a 'sort of studio in Pimlico, because Oliver gets so frightfully fed up with pins and yards of satin and ribbon and things all over the house'.

When she heard Clem was still looking for the right niche in life, Robina's green eyes lit with sudden excitement, then she launched into a flood of persuasion. Clem had always been wonderful at design in college, she said firmly, and, by the look of the dress she was wearing, still marvellous at making her own clothes. And Robina needed another brain. Not just someone to do the donkey-work, but a friend who could share in the the designing and take over when Oliver wanted his wife at his side in the Royal Enclosure at Ascot, or for a bit of shooting in Scotland. And of course, she added, the arrangement could be just as elastic and convenient for Miss Clemency Vaughan in return if she were sensible enough to accept the offer.

At first Clem had been doubtful. Sewing had been something she did solely because it was cheaper to make her own clothes. But it was also something she enjoyed doing, she admitted, and in the end Robina's enthusiasm proved so infectious that Clem found herself agreeing to attend a certain London establishment where well-connected young ladies were taught the finer points of sewing, including the virtues of perfect finishing, the requisite hallmark of the expert dressmaker's craft.

'You can do the rest, anyway,' said Robina, and smiled jubilantly. 'And this place Oliver's bought for me in Pimlico is such fun—flowers everywhere and baby-blue telephones. You'll love it.'

And Clem did. After she'd completed her crash course in fine sewing, she joined Robina in her smart little studio and very soon found that this new way to earn her living was one she thoroughly enjoyed. The design side of the business appealed strongly, as expected, but Clem rapidly developed a particular talent of her own that became the hallmark of a Robina Crichton creation. Clem found she possessed not only a talent for the exquisite embroidery Robina required, but an absolute genius for the creation of lifelike silk flowers to embellish the dramatic Victorian and eighteenth-century designs popular with Robina's clients for the ballgowns and wedding dresses they commissioned.

'You look seedy,' observed Robina, when Clem returned to the fold the following Monday. 'What can I order for you, darling? Tea, coffee, aspirin?'

'Just work, Robina. Lots of it.' Clem smiled bleakly. 'My energies are in sore need of channelling. So wheel it all out.'

Robina looked troubled, but as usual asked no questions. 'All right, darling. How about ten bridesmaids, one bride and one bride's mother for starters?'

'Perfect.'

The work helped. Long hours in company with other people while she worked her fingers to the bone on the Sheringham wedding 'set' were an anodyne which blunted a little of Clem's anguish. Emma and Jane were usually there in the evening in Putney when she got home, which was another form of help. Clem's carefully erected barrier of brittle gaiety deflected the questions it was obvious they were burning to ask, but after the first terse statement that Nicholas Wood was history, nothing more was said; not even when a parcel arrived for Clem addressed in Nick's scrawl, and contained only some freshly laundered underwear, and a single gold hoop earring. Clem suffered a serious setback in her recovery programme that day, but somehow survived the night by sole courtesy of her temper, since she spent the dark, hot hours cursing a man who could make love to her one minute as though his very life depended on it, then tell her to get lost almost in the next breath.

At first Clem had been convinced her heart was broken. In those first moments after Nick had hung up on her she had genuinely experienced an odd cessation of her life force, as though his words had been arrows which had pierced a vital organ. But as time wore on she came to acknowledge and give credit to the resilience of the human animal. Recovery was slow, admittedly, but recover she did, by telling herself over and over again that one week out of her life was not to be allowed to ruin the rest of it. Sometimes she longed to move from Putney, it was true, to leave the place that was such a short distance from Nick's own particular home ground. But stubborn resentment always changed her mind. Why should she move? Even if they did meet—so what?

Clem's recovery was slow and hard-won, but fairly well-established by the time she got home one night to find Emma and Jane preparing a meal minus Hamish and Don, their respective loved ones, which was a relief. Clem had no yen for male company at the end of a hard working day, and was grateful for the plate of microwaved tagliatelli thrust in her hand by Emma while Jane switched on a video she'd found pushed to the back of the bookshelf.

'I recorded *Singing in the Rain* ages ago,' said Emma with satisfaction. 'We'd forgotten all about it.'

The film was exactly the entertainment Clem needed after a long day dealing with a bride who had proved very difficult at her first fitting, and demanded several alterations to the style of the dress originally chosen. Clem laughed with the others, and enjoyed the inimitable dancing of Gene Kelly as always, and felt restored enough afterwards to volunteer for washing-up duty as the credits rolled up the screen at the end of the film. Jane dried dishes with Clem in the kitchen, leaving Emma to rewind the video, when suddenly a scream from the parlour sent Clem and Jane dashing to find out what was wrong. They found Emma with the remote control in her hand, her finger on the rewind button.

'Clem,' she said urgently, 'take a look at this.'

Mystified, Clem stared at the screen as a lady newsreader informed them about a news item several months old.

'Why are we watching an ancient newscast, for heaven's sake?' she demanded.

'Sh!' said Emma, her eyes fixed on the screen. 'It came on after the film—look!'

The scene switched from the newsdesk to a hot, dusty location, with sporadic shooting going on in the background and people running in all directions as vehicles exploded and the voice of the reporter sounded breathless, as though he'd been running too. Breathless and familiar. In sheer disbelief Clem stared at the tall figure of the reporter in thin cotton shirt and khaki trousers as he described the riot going on in the background. His face was sweating and smeared with dust, but unscarred, and both his eyes were perfectly normal, but the mop of untidy black hair and bony face were unmistakable. Clem hardly took in what he was saying, her eyes incredulous as he finished with, 'This is Nick Wood for the nine o'clock news——' Then the screen went blank and Emma rounded on Clem in excitement.

'That's where the timer stopped the video,' she said. 'But did you see Nick? Did you know about——'

'Oh yes, I saw.' Clem's eyes sparked with anger. 'But I didn't know about the rest. Nick has this thing about keeping certain areas of his life private. He really meant it, didn't he? I naturally thought he was a newspaper reporter.'

'No wonder we felt we knew him,' said Jane. 'We must have seen him dozens of times, only without the black patch and the scar. He looks a lot different without them, doesn't he?'

Clem snatched the remote control from Emma and rewound the video to the newscast again, freezing it at the point where Nick began to speak. She stared at his unscarred face, while her two friends looked on uneasily. 'So that's the sense of recognition I felt,' she said slowly. 'What a let-down!' She pressed the rewind button and sat down abruptly on the couch. 'I really believed he was the man I'd been waiting for all my life, you know. And all the time it was just because he was a face on a television screen. His name didn't mean anything. Because it's short and ordinary, I suppose.'

'Let's have a drink,' said Emma briskly, her eyes meeting Jane's in dismay.

'I'd rather have tea,' Clem smiled wryly. 'Sorry to be such a wet blanket these days.'

'Nonsense,' said Jane, while Emma went off to make the tea. 'Men can be such swine.'

'And women such lunatics over them. Well, no more of that for me. I'll settle for being an aunt to my nieces and nephews from now on, and leave the domestic bit to you ladies lucky enough to find nice, straightforward mates.'

'Sounds dull and unexciting, put like that.' Emma handed her a mug of tea.

Clem laughed. 'Sound and reliable, not dull. I can't imagine either Hamish or Don hugging dark secrets to their respective bosoms.' Nor telling their ladies to get lost either, she added to herself, depressed.

'You could do with a holiday,' said Jane. 'When are you off to Spain?'

'I was going to leave it until Chatty and Luiz were less busy towards the end of the season, but I think I've changed my mind. They rarely let their private villa, even if the hotel's full, so there'll probably be some corner for me to squeeze into.' Clem drank her tea and got up. 'I'll ring Charity now, then book a flight to Gerona if she says yes. I'll have finished my part of the Sheringham wedding set soon.'

Clem's arrangements were soon made. Charity

was only too delighted, and Robina perfectly amenable to the change of plan.

'As long as you're back in time for my cruise with Oliver, darling, off you go. Enjoy yourself. Stop eating your heart out for whoever it is you're eating your heart out for.'

When everything was arranged Clem had just under three weeks to finish the embroidery on the Sheringham bridal gown, make herself a couple of dresses and go down to Llanhowell for a weekend somewhere in the middle. After two days of cosseting by her mother, and pointed advice on looking after herself properly from her father, Clem returned to Putney in the rain on the Sunday evening to find Emma prowling up and down, waiting for her as she let herself in.

'He's been here,' blurted Emma, pouncing on her.

Clem's eyebrows rose. 'Good evening, Emma, and thank you, I've had a very nice weekend, Emma, and just exactly *who's* been here?'

'Nick.'

Clem blinked, and turned away quickly to hide the sudden breathlessness that hit her. 'How extraordinary. What did he want?'

Emma sighed in exasperation. 'To see you, of course!'

Clem sat down on the bottom stair and thought this over. After weeks of misery, followed by a period of hard-won calm, she found that her major reaction to the news was resentment. 'Good thing I was out, then, wasn't it, because I certainly don't want to see *him*!' She jumped to her feet as the doorbell rang, staring at Emma accusingly.

'I told him you'd be home later,' confessed the other girl, biting her lip.

'Then *you* can open the door, my fine friend. Because I'm going to bed.' And Clem hoisted her weekend bag and marched upstairs, slamming her bedroom door behind her. She unpacked angrily, flinging clothes about and banging drawers to drown out the sound of the deep male voice downstairs in conversation with Emma.

A knock on the door made her heart miss a beat, but it was Emma who peeped round the door, looking utterly miserable.

'It's Nick. He won't go away.'

'Oh, won't he?' Clem brushed past her friend and marched downstairs like an avenging angel, her eyes glittering like blue diamonds as she glared at the man watching her. He looked tired, and even thinner than before, the eye-patch replaced now by dark glasses which successfully hid any expression in the eyes watching her from behind them.

'Hello, Clemency,' he said quietly.

'Why are you here?' Clem stood very erect, half-way down the stairs.

'Because I couldn't stay away any longer.' His voice grated, as though the admission hurt him to make it.

'Is that supposed to be of any interest to me?' Clem managed to keep her voice light—conversational almost, as though the sight of him wasn't breaking her in pieces. 'As I remember it, you told me to stay out of your life. And I have.'

'I was out of my skull with jealousy when I said that.' Nick threw out a hand in an awkward gesture, obviously very conscious of Emma in the background. 'Look—couldn't we talk somewhere?'

'No.'

The single negative dropped like a gauntlet flung down between them, and Nick stepped back, hunching his shoulders.

'Clemency——'

'Please go.' Clem stood rigid, her face cold as she stared down at him from her vantage point. 'If you had an apology in mind for—for ruining my father's birthday, it would have been more acceptable if you'd made it nearer the time. It's too late now.'

'I've been in hospital.' He took off the sunglasses and turned his face up towards her. 'They did some work on the eyelid and tidied up the scar.'

Clem viewed the result woodenly. 'So I see. Quite an improvement. No doubt it was necessary—because of your particular livelihood, I mean.'

His mouth twisted as he replaced the glasses. 'So you've remembered where you saw me before, I take it. Nick Wood, television reporter.'

'Why did you think it necessary to hide the fact?' she asked before she could stop herself.

He shrugged morosely. 'You may find it hard

to believe, but some women rather like the idea of being seen with someone like me. Because my face appears on television, I mean.'

'Really?'

His teeth showed fleetingly in a humourless smile. 'But none of them fancied me as a disfigured, *retired* television reporter.'

'You choose the wrong companions.'

He nodded. 'How right you are!'

Clem clenched her teeth, stung by his tone. 'From which I gather you count me as one of the number.'

Nick shook his head. 'No. As I must have said before, several times, you are unique. And if I never mentioned the precise nature of my occupation, I suppose I wanted you to 1-like *me*, Nick Wood the man. Not Nick Wood the television reporter.'

'I don't really care who you are. I've had time to think since I saw you last, and I've decided first impressions are the most important, after all. If ever I *do* think of you—which isn't often—I'm inclined to remember the Beast.' Clem turned to go upstairs, but Nick sprang to the newel-post, looking up urgently into her cold face.

'Tell me who he was, Clemency!'

She stared at him blankly. 'Who are you talking about?'

'The man who was kissing you that night.' Nick reached up and seized her hands. 'I've got to know. It's killing me, wondering who the hell he is.'

Clem pulled away, eyeing him with distaste. 'You're mad. Or confusing me with someone else. I don't go round kissing every man I run into.'

'Perhaps your conduct in my own case misled me,' he said cruelly.

She went pale. 'Get out! Now!'

Nick reached up and caught her wrist, pulling her down forcibly until she was on a level with him. 'Not until you tell me who you were kissing in that bloody garage that night.'

Clem began to feel genuinely frightened. She tried to twist away, but Nick held her in a bruising grip. 'Emma!' she screamed. 'Call the police—tell them we've got an intruder, and he's assaulting me!'

Nick cursed and dropped her hand. 'So you'd set the law on me,' he said bitterly.

'Do you blame me?' She tossed back her hair, glaring at him. 'Besides, think how convenient it would be. You could report the incident yourself—get the cameras here. Nick Wood, for the nine o'clock news, Putney.'

'You're right about one thing,' he snapped. 'I *must* be mad—to love a woman like you.' And before she could stop him he pulled her into his arms and kissed her savagely, one hand wound in her hair to hold her still as his lips and tongue played havoc with hers. She was panting for breath when he finally flung her away from him and strode out of the house, banging the door behind him.

'Glory!' said Emma in awe as she crept down to Clem. 'Are you all right, love?'

Clem nodded dumbly, then screamed as the door flew open again.

Jane stood looking from one to the other, breathing hard. 'Nick Wood nearly knocked me over as he stormed down the path out there. What on earth's been going on?'

'You may well ask!' said Clem unsteadily, then began to laugh as Emma launched into an explanation. To her horror Clem found she couldn't stop laughing, and went on and on until Jane slapped her face and told her to cry for once like other people, and Emma held her tight for a while until she was calm.

'You know,' said Clem hoarsely at last, as the three of them downed large glasses of medicinal vodka spiked with orange juice, 'Hugo was a lot less trouble, one way and another.'

Emma agreed, sighing. 'But I just can't picture Hugo kissing you senseless like that. I came over quite peculiar just watching you.'

'Damn, damn!' said Jane bitterly. 'Why didn't I come home earlier? I missed all the best bits!'

At which Clem started to laugh again, but in genuine amusement this time, and the other two joined in, relieved to see her rational again.

'One thing though, you two,' said Clem soberly, as they went up to bed. 'I don't suppose for a moment that he will, but if by any strange chance Nick Wood comes here again, just shut the door in his face. Don't let him in. Don't tell him anything about me. Don't even say hello.'

'Are you sure?' Emma looked wistful.

Clem paused in her bedroom doorway. 'Yes, perfectly sure.'

But afterwards she lay awake for half the night, tossing and turning at the thought of those few moments when Nick's arms and mouth had taken her by surprise. Her brain told her to be sensible, to pretend the incident had never happened, but her body refused to go along with the idea, reminding her that her bruised mouth tingled, and her ribs hurt where he had crushed her in his arms, and quite shamelessly made it clear it longed to undergo the same sweet punishment all over again.

Clem had a lot to make up as far as her recovery programme was concerned after Nick's visit. Seeing Nick again had made it humiliatingly plain that she was only immune to him, it seemed, as long as she never laid eyes on him. The moment he'd appeared on her own doorstep, her carefully built carapace of indifference had disintegrated, leaving her as vulnerable to him as she'd ever been.

To make matters worse, from then on fate seemed to take infinite delight in conspiring against her. Only a day or two later Clem met Nick face to face as she hurried out of East Putney Underground on her way home. She flushed bright red, his face went a sickly colour under his faded tan, then she brushed past him in the crowd and made for home as if the hounds of hell were after her. She kept quiet about the incident to Emma and Jane, hoping that by pretending Nick didn't exist she might somehow get over him faster. She carefully avoided all the places they were likely to meet, which meant no more Sunday strolls in Fulham Palace Gardens, or an occasional drink in the White Horse in Parson's Green, though a trip to the cinema with Emma seemed safe enough one evening, since Clem knew Nick was by no means a regular cinemagoer. Her luck was out. As Clem and Emma went out into the hot summer night, discussing the film they'd just seen, they almost collided with Nick and a very pretty girl who never even noticed that her escort stiffened and tried to accost the fair, beautiful girl who swept past him, her stony blue eyes cutting him dead.

'Gosh, that was Nick,' said Emma, craning her neck to look behind her.

'Yes.'

'With a very attractive companion too.'

Clem glared at her friend. 'Do you think I didn't notice?'

'Well, you *did* tell him to push off, Clem.'

'Oh, shut up, Em!'

'Sorry.'

At the weekend Clem went shopping with Jane in the King's Road. She wanted a birthday present for her brother Penry, and spent a pleasant morning browsing through the fashionable shops with her friend before buying an ultra-large sweater in Hackett's.

'A bit pricey,' said Clem ruefully, as she left the shop clutching a stiff white paper carrier bag. 'There's a lot of Penry to cover, unfortunately.'

Jane laughed, then broke off to examine a shirt in the window, wondering aloud if it would suit her Don. Clem peered at it over her shoulder, then felt a touch on her arm and turned quickly.

'Oh!' She stared up in dismay at a familiar scarred face, lost for further words for a moment until Nick seized her by the elbows, the touch of his fingers hot on her bare skin.

'Clemency——' he began urgently, but she jerked free of his grip and literally dragged an unwilling Jane away and made off at a tremendous rate, leaving Nick staring after them in anger.

'He's livid,' panted Jane, looking back.

'I should be sorry?' Clem strode blindly through passersby on the pavement, the unfortunate Jane, who was much shorter, hurrying after her as fast as she could.

'Couldn't you just have a talk with him?' gasped Jane. 'There may be a simple explanation of what happened.'

'Nothing happened. So what's to explain?'

Jane gave up. 'Oh, all right. Make a mess of your life—it's your life!'

And a very hard life it was for the moment, Clem found, as the chance meetings with Nick fanned what she had fondly believed to be the ashes of her feelings for him into bright, unendurable flames again. She worked like someone possessed during the day, hoping to tire herself out so she could sleep at night instead of physically yearning for Nick during the long, hot hours of darkness. It would pass, she told herself firmly. It was nothing to worry about. All she had to do was treat the episode with Nick like an illness that required a long convalescence and careful nursing to effect full recovery. To which end she applied herself to the new dresses she was making for herself in the evenings, and lived out the time until her departure for Spain with grim endurance, almost afraid to look about her in shops and in the street in case she laid eyes on Nick again and found herself back to square one.

'There's a tall, dark hunk of man asking if he can take you home,' said Robina gaily, as Clem was getting ready to leave the Pimlico studio one evening.

Clem swallowed hard, clenched her teeth and said: 'Tell him to get lost.'

Robina's eyebrows shot into her hair. 'Little quarrel, darling? If so I think you'd better tell him yourself, he's bigger than me. Anyway, I told him to come in and get you.'

'What's up with you, Clem?' demanded Dr Penry Vaughan, aggrieved, and relieved his sister of the large bag she was holding in front of her like a shield.

Clem sagged. 'Oh, it's you, Pen!'

'Well, thanks—I'm pleased to see you too.' Penry exchanged glances with Robina Crichton, who shrugged very slightly and laid a long fingernail against her lips for an instant.

'How *are* you, Penry, you gorgeous creature?' she said, smiling. 'Still rocketing the nurses' blood pressure in your temple of healing?'

'Certainly not,' he retorted primly. 'Penry the Pure, they call me.'

Clem had recovered enough to give him a sisterly shove as they took leave of Robina. 'Penry the Pain, you mean. Does this unexpected honour mean I'm obliged to feed you tonight?'

'Yes, please. Then I'll buy you a drink afterwards to say thank you.'

Once the humiliating shock of disappointment receded, Clem brightened at the prospect of an evening with her brother, who was a great favourite with Emma and Jane. When Clem let herself into the house, the two girls were in the kitchen. They exclaimed in delight at the sight of Penry, and Jane promptly tossed another packet of spaghetti in the pot, while Emma threw more bacon and tomatoes, and anything else she could think of, into the sauce she was concocting.

'This is what I call a meal,' said Penry blissfully, as he polished off a second helping of pasta, accompanied by the last of the outsize salad. 'Great food, and three beautiful women to eat it with.'

'And everything free!' said Clem drily.

He rolled his smoke-blue eyes at Emma and Jane. '*Everything*?'

They both giggled and plied him with chocolate cake, followed by a hunk of cheese to eat with most of the loaf of bread intended for the following morning's breakfast toast.

'Food and sparkling conversation's all you get,' said Jane, not without a trace of regret on her pretty face as she smiled at Penry.

'Ah, well,' he said philosophically, 'one mustn't be greedy. Let me take you out to the White Horse for a drink, girls, as a token of my deep appreciation.'

'No,' said Clem involuntarily.

Penry eyed her searchingly. 'No drink?'

'No White Horse. Couldn't we go somewhere else?'

'Sorry, Sis. Said I'd meet a chap there.'

'Then I'll sit this one out.' Clem got up and took a tray of used plates into the kitchen. Emma and Jane followed her to help.

'You can't stay in for ever just because you're afraid to bump into Nick,' said Emma, forthright as usual.

'No. But I can until I get back from Spain. Until my armour's stronger.' Clem went on swishing china through the detergent bubbles.

'I thought I'd come out this evening too,' said Jane casually as she wielded a tea-towel. 'If you go, that is.'

'*I* can't,' said Emma, and fixed Clem with a straight look, 'because Hamish is coming round later.'

Clem sighed, resigned. 'I see. And if Jane and I leave you in peace for a change, you and Hamish can have a private little orgy on your own.'

'Hamish isn't into orgies,' said Emma regretfully. 'But we haven't had much time to ourselves lately, now you come to mention it.'

Clem knew when she was beaten, and went upstairs to change into a white-spotted blue shirt and white cotton trousers, gathering her hair up on top of her head in a loose knot tied with a blue ribbon. Jane, who was small and brown-haired, sighed as Clem sent Penry to tidy up.

'I wish I had your looks, Clem.'

'You're welcome to them, as far as I'm concerned!'

Jane looked unconvinced, but brightened, smoothing down her yellow dress as Penry reappeared.

'Where's Don tonight?' said Clem in her ear.

Jane turned blank eyes on her, as though she'd forgotten who Don was. 'Oh—he's off on a course for a couple of days.'

Clem was on pins as the three of them threaded their way through the crowded tables on the pavement outside the White Horse in Parson's Green. She sighed with relief once they were inside. No familiar dark head was among the crowd. Penry pointed out an empty table on the raised platform in the corner, and sent the girls to take possession of it while he went off to the bar.

'You Vaughans are a striking lot,' said Jane, as she watched Penry laughing with one of the barmen. 'Penry's a very attractive hunk of male, Clem.'

Clem shot an uneasy look at her friend, rather

alarmed by Jane's expression as she gazed after Penry. It could hardly be described as suitable for the face of a girl due to walk up the aisle with another man in the not so distant future. Then she remembered one of Jane's remarks and kept quiet. If was Jane's life, after all. And an innocent hour in a pub with her friend's brother could hardly be described as infidelity, even if the absent Don did happen to suffer a bit in contrast to young Dr Vaughan, both in size and looks. And who was she anyway, thought Clem in derision, to put her oar in anyone else's love-life when her own was in such a mess? She chatted with Jane while they waited, trying to ignore the pain she felt inside. Her last visit to the place had been with Nick, and this fact dominated her mind to such an extent she hardly knew what Jane was talking about. It was a relief when Penry came back, juggling with a pint of beer and two glasses of lager.

'My chum isn't here yet,' he announced as he folded his considerable length into a chair. He smiled at Jane wickedly over his beer. 'Do you come here often?'

She giggled. 'I think there's a rude answer to that!'

Jane's eyes sparkled as Penry flirted with her, and Clem looked on absently, comforting herself with the thought that in a few days she would be in Spain, where she could stop looking over her shoulder all the time, in constant fear—and hope, she realised unhappily, of meeting Nick everywhere.

'I say,' said Penry, who sat facing the bar, 'there's a chap over there who looks familiar.'

'One of your medical men?'

'No.' Penry frowned, thinking hard, then shook his head. 'Can't place him, yet I know him, I'm sure.'

'Maybe he's an actor,' said Jane.

'Whoever he is, he's certainly interested in me,' said Penry, grinning.

'Perhaps he fancies you!' Jane chuckled, and craned her neck to see over the crowd.

Clem went cold. She kept her back turned and swallowed some of her drink swiftly.

'He certainly doesn't fancy me,' said Penry. 'In fact, if looks could kill——'

'Oh dear,' said Jane. 'It's not you he's interested in, Penry.'

'You haven't been been doing naughties behind your Don's back, by any chance, Jane?' Penry smiled at her reprovingly, then his eyes narrowed at the anxious look on her face.

'It's Nick, Clem,' said Jane in a small voice.

Clem nodded, resigned, and stared into her drink. 'I thought it might be.'

Penry demanded enlightenment, but received only as much as Clem thought fit to provide. She gave a quick look in the direction Jane described, and decided she could make it through the nearest door, since Nick was standing by the bar at a point near the farther exit.

'I think I'll make a run for it,' she said. 'I can get

a taxi home.'

'Look,' said Penry, 'if you want me to sort this chap out, Clem——'

'God forbid! It's the last thing I want.' She turned to Jane. 'Go to the loo, Jane, and say hello to Nick on the way back. Keep him talking while I get away.'

Jane looked appalled at the prospect, but reluctantly went off to do as Clem wanted.

Penry subjected his sister to a very close scrutiny. 'Hurt badly, love?' he asked quietly, and Clem nodded, touched by his unaccustomed gentleness.

'Yes. But I'll get over it.' She kept an eye on Jane, who was making her way towards the spot where Nick was talking to the young Australian barman Clem remembered from another, happier time. 'Right, I'm off now, Pen. Will you see Jane home, please? In one piece, preferably,' she added with meaning.

Penry nodded, and stood up to kiss her, giving her a hug as she braced herself for escape. 'I'll sort this chap out for you gladly, you know.'

'No, thanks, I'll do my own sorting out.' Clem smiled up at her young brother affectionately, put a hand to his cheek, then slipped away as quickly as possible, only to run into Jane on her way to the door.

'You can come back to the table now,' her friend informed her. 'I barely had time to say hello to Nick before he saw you and Penry. He looked absolutely murderous, then muttered goodnight to me and dashed off. So there's not much point in your doing likewise, love. Come and have another drink.'

Clem nodded glumly, because she knew how much Jane wanted her to, but it took all her strength of will to stay chatting and laughing with the other two, and later to make an effort to be pleasant to Penry's colleague when he put in an appearance. It was late before the foursome broke up, the young men to get back to their flat near the hospital, the girls to Putney in a taxi. When they arrived Jane went on into the house, leaving Clem to settle with the taxi-driver, feeling decidedly worn.

'Don't go in yet,' said a deep voice, as she turned to go up the path.

The hair on her neck stood up, and she bit back a scream as a hand reached in front of her in the darkness and closed the front door very quietly. She whirled round to face Nick, who took her by the elbows and held her fast, looming over her forbiddingly.

'And who was *this* one?' he said very softly, his fingers biting into her skin. 'Tell me—to the nearest figure—just how many men you need, Clemency?'

Clem was frightened, and angry with herself because of it. She raised her chin and met his angry eyes squarely. 'It can hardly matter to you who I go out with, or drink with, or—or kiss. As I remember it, you told me to stay out of your life. And I have. So I'd be much obliged if you'd return the compliment, Nicholas Wood, and stay out of mine!'

'Who was he?' he snarled, ignoring her.

'My *brother*!' Clem tried to shake his hands off as he gave a savage bark of laughter.

'Oh, come on, Clemency, you can do better than that!'

'It may come as a surprise to you, but I don't *have* to do anything. I'm my own woman.'

'Unfortunately for my peace of mind—and body—I can't rid myself of the feeling that you're mine.' He bent and kissed her hard, but her mouth stayed closed and unyielding as she stiffened in outrage in his arms. He lifted his mouth a fraction. 'No response?' he muttered against her lips. 'Would it help if I abased myself completely, Clemency, told you I was willing to go against every principle I've ever lived by just to have you in my bed again?' He let out a long, unsteady breath, and tightened his arms, subduing the sudden lunge she made to break free. 'No, you don't. I want you to listen to me. What I'm trying to say is that I've come to a very soul-destroying conclusion. I can't live like this. I want you so much, I'm willing to turn a blind eye—appropriately enough—to any occasional lapses on your part, if only you'll come back to me.'

Clem felt sick. She fought the nausea down, drops of perspiration pearling her upper lip as she clenched her teeth.

'Well?' he demanded hoarsely, shaking her a little. 'God almighty, Clemency, what more do you want me to say? Isn't it enough for you to see me reduced to this?'

She shuddered. 'What you suggest is an insult, to us both. You must be drunk!'

'Not drunk—demented.' And he crushed her to him and kissed her until she clutched him to keep her balance, her mouth opening to gasp for air, and he gave an exultant laugh and kissed her parted lips in triumph, his tongue seducing her into shaming response. Clem shook with rage at herself and pushed at him, but Nick was lost in a desire so introspected that he seemed blind and deaf to anything but the feel of her body against his. Then his fingers slid to the buttons on her shirt and Clem seized the advantage. Her sudden, eel-like wriggle took him by surprise, and somehow she managed to twist out of his grasp and lunge for the door, which opened as she reached it and sent her sprawling on her hands and knees on the hall carpet, to the astonishment of Jane, who'd come to see where she was.

'My God, Clem, what happened?' she demanded, helping her up. 'Did you lock yourself out? I heard the door close and thought you'd gone straight up to your room, then Em just said you weren't there and I panicked . . .' She trailed into silence as she caught sight of the man outside.

'I got waylaid,' panted Clem, and turned on Nick, staring at him balefully. 'Why don't you just go?'

Nick stood looking down at her, his fists clenched. The hall light threw his scar into cruel relief, and for a moment Clem's heart contracted, then he put out a hand in appeal, and she stepped back deliberately.

'Clemency——'

'Just go,' she said, in a voice so deadly quiet his head went up as though she'd struck him. 'Tomorrow, when you're sober, you'll be sorry you sullied your precious principles by the offer you just made.'

Emma was peering over Jane's shoulder, and both girls' eyes opened wide at this.

'And glad,' went on Clem inexorably, 'that I rejected it. And you.' She gave the still man a look of cold disdain, then turned her back on him and went upstairs, leaving Nicholas to bid Emma and Jane a punctilious goodnight, and to apologise for his intrusion before he walked away into the warm summer night.

As they locked up, Jane and Emma had a whispered discussion about whether to ask Clem if she needed tea, or sympathy, but in the end decided privacy was their friend's major requirement, and left her alone to enjoy it. Not that 'enjoy' was an apt term, because Clem lay awake all night long, racked by misery over Nick's humiliating proposal.

It was, she decided, staring out at the stars, a very mortifying thing to be wanted by a man just because he had an urge to possess her body; an urge so strong, moreover, that he was actually prepared to share her with the mythical 'others' of his imagination. And the great joke of it all was that, in spite of all the things he'd said, she still loved the man. Clem sat bolt upright in bed, pushing her damp hair away from her neck as the truth struck home. It *was* true, she thought, panicking, and slid out of bed and went downstairs to get a drink. Almost immediately the other bedroom doors opened and Emma and Jane went running downstairs after her.

'Are you all right?' they asked in unison, and Clem laughed shakily and offered them some of the orange juice she was pouring.

'I just had a collision with the truth, that's all. And it hurt.'

'Is there anything we can do?' asked Jane anxiously.

Clem's eyes softened. 'No. My problem is simple. It took me all these years to fall in love, and then when I did I chose the wrong man. Mind you, I suppose I should be flattered. Not many men would be willing to take on a woman with all faults, so to speak, which was the gist of Nick's offer tonight.'

Emma frowned as she poured juice into two glasses. 'Would we be horribly inquisitive if we said we're dying to know just what these "faults" of yours are supposed to be?'

'Search me. God knows, I'm not perfect, but for some reason Nicholas Wood thinks I'm first cousin to the whore of Babylon.' Clem smiled wryly. 'Funny, isn't it, when I'm really just an old-fashioned one-man girl.'

'So Nick thinks you've got a couple of interests

on the side, then?'

'Certainly does. One of whom he saw kissing me in the White Horse tonight.'

Jane groaned. 'Oh Lord! Didn't you tell Nick it was your brother?'

Clem shrugged. 'He didn't believe a word of it. He's obsessed by some outsize bee in his bonnet about my liberal tendencies towards his sex.'

'So what now?' asked Emma.

'I go to Spain. Where I can relax, and where Nicholas Wood won't be popping up in front of me wherever I go.' Clem downed her orange juice. 'Only first I've got a wedding dress to finish, and if I don't rest my weary eyes for a while, Miss Annabel Sheringham is likely to find some very peculiar motifs embroidered across her aristocratic bosom!'

CHAPTER SIX

A FEW days later Clem lay supine in the early morning sun on the tiny beach exclusive to the Villa Isabel near the village of Cabo Feliz, on the coast not far from Gerona. Her nieces, *las senoritas* Dolores and Luiza Santana, were sitting at her feet, absorbed in the jigsaw puzzles their aunt had brought them from London. Clem watched them from under the brim of her white cotton hat, enchanted by the grave consideration the little girls accorded each large wooden piece as they tried to fit it into the pattern, her eyes soft as they rested on the two curly blonde heads.

'*Hola*, Clem,' called a husky voice, and Clem sat up, smiling, to wave at Milagrita Carreras, Luiz's cousin, who had arrived the night before. She was picking her way over the pebbles, looking elegant as always, in a filmy shirt knotted over a perfectly cut one-piece bathing-suit.

'*Tia, Tia!*' clamoured the little girls, who rushed to lift their faces for the kisses their Spanish aunt rained down on them.

'And how are you today?' asked Milagrita, settling herself on the sunbed beside Clem.

'I'm very well.'

'*Es verdad?*'

'Yes, truly.' Clem smiled, and began to rub oil

113

into her long brown legs. 'I haven't been ill, you know.'

'No. Only the lovesickness.' The grey eyes were shrewd. 'And when love comes late, it comes hard, *querida*. I have watched you. Sometimes you are sad. He must be *mucho hombre*, this man of yours.'

'He's not mine.' Clem kept her eyes on the blue, blue sea, and pulled her hat low on her forehead. 'Let's not talk about him. Tell me about Juan instead.'

'Juan is busy, as always, but he will drive down from Granada this weekend.' Milagrita smiled serenely. 'I do not leave him often, but I thought I would like to see for myself how you are.'

'I'm flattered!'

'Also, I thought you might need some company because Charity is so busy at this time of the year.'

'Thank you—I'm grateful. Not that I'm lonely, of course, with these two charmers for company, but I do tend to worry about Chatty a bit. Should she be doing so much now she's pregnant again?'

Milagrita shrugged. 'I think she does far more than Luiz wishes, but she is so proud of this hotel of theirs. It is their baby too, I think. They have worked so hard together for its success.'

Clem agreed, remembering how Luiz had seized the chance of owning his own hotel, after years of managing his uncle's in Marbella, as he had done when he had first met Charity.

'At least they've got the villa to come home to

at night,' said Clem. 'And Chatty's promised to spend the rest of the day with us today, once lunch is over at the hotel.'

'Now I am here she can spend the rest of the week with you, *chica. I* shall help in the hotel.' Milagrita smiled in triumph.

Clem's face lit up. *'Really?* I offered to lend a hand myself, but Chatty and Luiz wouldn't hear of it.'

'I shall enjoy it. Do not forget, I was brought up to the hotel business, Clemency. My name is not "Little Miracle" for nothing!' Milagrita laughed, then settled herself comfortably under the big striped umbrella. 'Now, tell me all the news about Kit and my old friend Reid, and their beautiful sons, also the so charming Penry, that heartbreaker of a brother of yours!'

The morning passed pleasantly and quickly until it was time to take the little girls up to join their mother at the villa for lunch on the vine-framed patio. Afterwards Clem was adamant her sister had a rest.

'Since Milagrita has volunteered so nobly for duty, I just might,' yawned Charity. 'I get so sleepy when I'm pregnant. Come on, my darlings, siesta time.' She rounded up her little daughters, then eyed Clem. 'And what about you? Any plans for this afternoon? I'll be up and around again by four or so.'

Clem's programme was to return to the beach, swim a little, lie in the shade and read or doze. 'I shall wallow in sheer laziness,' she said, stretching luxuriously. 'I've been working like a maniac these past few weeks.'

'Sounds as though Robina's running a sweatshop!'

'Not a bit of it. She's a dear, actually. We get on surprisingly well together. And believe me, she's no dummy when it comes to business. She can tell at a glance what suits a client best.' Clem giggled. 'She has her work cut out sometimes, when a well-upholstered chum fancies skin-tight satin bristling with beads, but in the end the lady always goes away convinced the flattering black chiffon, or whatever, was her own idea in the first place, and everyone's happy.'

'Robina always was a bossy soul.' Charity laughed and kissed her sister, then shepherded her daughters off to rest.

With Milagrita's help the days soon took on a pleasant routine. Clem insisted on taking charge of the children during the early part of the morning, then Charity joined them on the beach for an hour or two before lunch, after which she took her daughters off to bed for a rest, adamant that Clem had the afternoon to herself. The student son of the head waiter, Luiz discovered, was only too glad to earn some money by acting as Clem's chauffeur and guide on her expeditions into the neighbouring countryside, since Cabo Feliz itself offered little in the way of diversion apart from the hotel itself, which, though beautiful, possessed one main disadvantage from Clem's point of view.

The Hostal Isabella, situated in the centre of the village itself was over a century old, and had once been a *hidalgo's* country residence. It was built around a central cobbled patio with a fountain, with geraniums in splashes of red and green against walls decked with the frivolous black lace of iron balconies. Luiz was too much the experienced hotelier not to exploit the commercial possibilities of his hotel to the full, but at the same time he took great care to maintain its gracious, old-world atmosphere, using the original *sala* of the old house for his reception area, where the great curving staircase was only one among many features which brought visitors back to the hotel year after year, pleased by the efficient courtesy of the staff and the charm of the owner and his beautiful wife. But Clem had learned early on during her first visits that it was best to keep away from the hotel on her own, purely to avoid the inevitable confusion over her resemblance to Charity.

José, or Pepe, as he asked Clem to call him, was a dark-eyed, rather serious boy, who spoke enough English to make their daily excursions very pleasant, and because he was a history student he took great pride in showing his companion as many monuments, Romanic churches and monasteries as she could take in, until she begged for mercy at last and proposed an afternoon spent in Gerona itself. The trip was a great success. Pepe parked the car on the north side of the town near the park, only five minutes

away from the old quarter, and Clem followed
obediently as he conducted her to the places he
considered most important. She enjoyed the bustle
of a busy city again after days of sea and sand, but
was resigned to a visit to the cathedral first before
Pepe would allow anything more mundane. After
paying due respect to the grand approach of the
edifice and its enormously wide nave, Clem was
able to wander with a free heart through the
fascinating lanes of the city, to climb up steep steps
and peer through arches, to inspect the Arabic
baths and the medieval Jewish quarter, and take
photographs of the painted houses which rose
straight up from the banks of the River Oñar.

After the urban delights of Gerona, Pepe thought
they should return to the scenic delights of the
coast next day and drove Clem past curving
beaches and pine-encrusted bays to Cadaques, the
St Tropez of Spain, where as a matter of course, by
this time, she first inspected the baroque church
before wandering through the cobbled streets of the
town to gaze at the ancient roofs and whitewashed
walls of houses which Pepe informed her more
often than not contained architect-designed
interiors. And, since Pepe was adamant that the
senorita could not possibly leave the area without a
visit to Salvador Dali's house in Port Lligat before
returning to Cabo Feliz, it was a rather tired Clem
who finally arrived, yawning and apologetic, at the
villa later that evening.

Charity plied her with tea and questions about
the expedition, then handed Dolly and Luiza over

to Pilar for a while and took Clem upstairs to her bedroom.

'Just look at me,' said Charity disconsolately, waving a hand at her reflection in the full-length mirror. 'My waistline is quite definitely thickening already. It's happening sooner this time, Clem. Hardly any of my dresses fit me properly, but I really don't fancy getting into maternity gear just yet.'

Clem smiled soothingly. 'I may have just the answer.' She went off to her own room and returned with a dress. 'Try this. It's a sort of wrapover effect. Put it on like a coat, and tie it at one side, then presto, deep neckline—perfectly cut, I might add—flattering full skirt, and a waistline you can adjust as you go along.'

Charity's face lit with pleasure as she revolved in front of the mirror. 'It's perfect, Clem. Luiz will just love me in this!'

'No kidding!' Clem grinned. 'Keep it. And if you like, we'll get some dress lengths tomorrow, and I'll make you a couple more in return for my bed and board.'

Charity was indignant at the mere idea of any return, but accepted the offer when Clem insisted, hugging her twin before she took off the dress and pulled on a swimsuit.

'Come on, let's go down to the beach with Dolly and Luiza until their suppertime. Luiz is dragging Milagrita away from the reception desk later on and we'll have one of the chef's specials for dinner. I yearn for Franco's *huevos a la flamenca*—eggs baked with tomatoes, onions and diced ham to you, *cariad*, not to mention the asparagus and peppers and sausage he throws in—mm, yummy!'

'If having babies makes you eat all the time, I don't think I'll bother with the experience.' Clem stopped short, her eyes clouding, then she ran off ahead of Charity to collect her small nieces, making them shout with laughter at her sudden bear-hugs as she helped them into their bathing-suits. For the rest of the afternoon she was untiring in her efforts to entertain the children, playing ball with them on the shallow half-moon of sand beyond the pebbles, encouraging them with their tentative efforts at swimming, then reading to them in the shade from one of the pile of illustrated books she'd brought with her from England.

Charity joined in some of the games, just watched some of the others, and never said a word about the admiration she felt for this beloved other half of herself, who she knew only too well was still licking her wounds in private, behind the brave front put on for the world at large.

Not that Clem believed for a moment her act was deceiving Charity. The silver cord that bound them was too strong for successful subterfuge between them. But forbearance was given unquestioningly. Charity felt the hurt as if it were her own, Clem knew, but let it pass without comment, for which her twin was deeply grateful as they sat together on the beach watching the shadows cast by the umbrella pines as the sun headed for the sea, and the little girls squabbled a little over the books they were colouring, as bedtime grew nearer.

'They could almost be you and me at that age,' said Clem, after settling a dispute on whose crayons were whose. 'Only Dolly's older than Luiza, of course.'

'And we never squabbled over anything much.'

'True.'

They lounged in comfortable silence for a while, until Pilar, the young girl who helped with the children, could be seen making her way down from the house.

'It's high time *you* had a husband and children,' said Charity, gathering her children's belongings together. 'You can't go on making other people's wedding dresses all your life.'

'I don't see why not.' The identical pairs of blue eyes locked. 'I truly believe there's no alternative for me, Chatty. The only man I've ever wanted wants *me* for all the wrong reasons.'

'But surely you'll find someone else?'

'I don't want anyone else.'

'But you only spent six days with this man, Clem!'

Clem pulled on her shirt and stuffed her belongings in her bag. 'That's right. The Israelis had their six-day war, and I had my six days of love. More than some women ever have, perhaps.'

Charity looked almost ready to cry as the young maid reached them to carry off her daughters. '*Gracias*, Pilar.' She turned on Clem fiercely. 'This Nicholas Wood isn't the only man in the world!'

'I know that. But he's put me off the rest of his

sex, believe me. Luiz excepted, of course!'

Clem took longer to dress than usual that evening. The bedtime story her nieces chose was the longest they could find, so she was late having her shower and extra time was necessary to shampoo the salt from her hair. Not that it mattered much in Cabo Feliz. Everyone dined late anyway, and Luiz liked to make sure everything was in order at the hotel before he could relax with his wife over their own evening meal, which was by no means mere eating, but more in the nature of the main entertainment of the day, with plenty of wine and conversation to accompany the food. There was no set pattern to the menu. Sometimes Charity cooked dinner, sometimes it was sent down from the hotel, and occasionally it was provided by Luiz himself, when dinner was invariably a cold buffet, since where food was concerned Luiz was more by way of a chief than one of the Indians, Charity said, which somewhat mystified Milagrita.

As Clem dried her hair she could hear voices floating up from the patio below as Luiz and Charity relaxed together in the sea-scented dusk. She smiled a little wistfully and lingered deliberately in front of the mirror, taking her time before joining them. She felt rather pleased with her appearance, since in the time since her arrival her hair had become streaked by the sun like Charity's, and her eyes shone more deeply blue than ever in the deep gold of her face, even to her own clinical gaze. She put on one of the new dresses she'd made for herself, in thin black cotton, cut like the one given to Charity, but with a cluster of her own handmade white rosebuds at the waist instead of ties. The deep V-shaped neckline showed off her new tan rather well, she thought, pleased, as she fastened large white hoops in her ears. Then she frowned, startled, as she heard a sudden commotion from below. Angry voices were raised, then a scream came from Charity, followed by sounds of scuffling, and chairs being overturned.

Clem tore from the room, afraid someone had broken in, and flew downstairs to the patio, her eyes starting from her head at the scene confronting her in the dusk. Charity stood pressed against one of the vine-clad stone pillars, her hands to her mouth as she stared down at the body of an unconscious man, while Luiz stood over the intruder, fists clenched, still bristling with the rage that had obviously just driven him to knock the man down.

'What on earth is going on?' demanded Clem in alarm, hurrying over to her trembling sister. 'Hey! Steady—calm down now. Remember the baby.'

Luiz abandoned the body in the shadows and took his wife in his arms, smoothing her hair as he explained what had happened, since Charity seemed struck dumb for the moment with shock, and Clem bent to peer at the intruder, her heart flipping over in her chest as she realised who he was.

'I went upstairs to see the children,' Luiz said, his voice shaking with anger. 'I stay with them a little. When I come back a man is molesting my wife, so I hit him.' He released Charity reluctantly. '*Mi amor*, I must call the police.'

'No!' gasped Charity at last. 'He thought I was Clem, Luiz. That's why he tried to kiss me——'

By this time Clem was on her knees by the fallen man. 'I know him. It's Nick Wood. I-I think you've killed him, Luiz.'

There was a wail from Charity as Luiz thrust her aside to drop down beside Clem. He felt Nick's wrist and put an ear to his mouth, then let out an explosive sigh of relief. 'He breathes. I knocked him unconscious only. Help me move him.'

'Should he be moved? Maybe he's broken something.' Clem's voice was unsteady as Luiz ran his hands over the long body her own hands had once caressed with such pleasure.

'I think all is well. And if we get him to the sofa in the *sala* he will be more comfortable. Or shall I ring the hotel and get one of the waiters to come?' Luiz's worried grey eyes met Clem's questioningly, but she shook her head.

'No, let's not involve anyone else. I'll take his head and shoulders, you cope with the rest.'

Not without a struggle, they managed to manhandle Nick's slim, surprisingly heavy body inside to the *sala*, where Clem could see better. After a swift examination, her probing fingers found a contusion under the thick black hair at the back of his head.

'Must have knocked himself out when he fell on the tiles out there,' she said tersely, then gave Luiz a crooked smile. 'He'll have a fair bruise on his chin too, I shouldn't wonder, if the state of your knuckles is anything to go by.'

Charity flew to her husband to examine his bleeding hand, then took a long, hard look at the unconscious face of Nicholas Ward. 'So that's him,' she said, and turned apologetic blue eyes on her sister. 'He sort of materialised in front of me in the dark and frightened me out of my wits. Before I could scream or anything, he said 'Clemency!' and grabbed me and kissed me, and before I could say a word Luiz came, and pulled him off me and knocked him down.'

Luiz threw his hands out in despair. '*Lo siento*, Clem. But I believed he was attacking my wife. I felt murder in my heart, so I hit him.'

'You did indeed,' agreed Clem. 'I'll get some ice.'

'*Buenas tardes, amigos!*' Milagrita arrived in a cloud of perfume, her eyes like saucers at the sight of the recumbent figure on the sofa. '*Madre de Dios*, who is *that*?'

'Clemency's lover,' said Luiz, running a distracted hand over his hair.

'You have *killed* him?'

'No, no,' said Charity hurriedly, and switched to Spanish to explain, while Clem went off to the kitchen to collect ice from the freezer and a cloth to make a compress. She was on her way back when she heard sounds which seemed to indicate that Nick was coming round. She paused in the archway to the *sala*, watching from behind the sofa as Luiz helped his uninvited guest to sit up a little, while Charity put cushions behind his back.

Nick put a hand to his eyes, groaning. 'My God, what hit me?'

'I fear it was I,' said Luiz stiffly.

Some imp of perversity kept Clem where she was as Nick sat bolt upright, clutching his head as he stared at the muscular Spaniard. 'I've seen you before,' he said with hostility, and glared at Charity, who was hovering over him anxiously.

'It's time I introduced you. His name's Luiz Santana,' said Charity helpfully, and smiled. 'He's my husband.'

Nick's face turned a more ghastly colour than before. 'Your husband? Since when?'

'Seven years next month,' said Charity.

Clem held her breath as she watched Nick close his eyes and swallow hard, very obviously fighting with nausea for a moment before he struggled to his feet and stood swaying. Luiz put out a hand to support him, but Nick waved it away.

'I apologise for the intrusion, Senor Santana,' he said harshly. 'Also for—for subjecting your wife to——'

'Clem!' said Charity sharply. 'Will you get yourself over here and put the poor man out of his misery?'

Nick spun round as Clem came into the room, bearing her bundle of ice, his eyes starting from his head at the sight of her.

'Hello, Nick,' she said without emotion. 'Let me do something for that head.'

Nick stared wildly from Clem to Charity, then back again.

'*Caramba*!' said Milagrita in an undertone to Luiz. 'He did not know Clemency had a *gemela*, I think.'

'Didn't you ever think to mention me?' said Charity crossly.

'Oh yes, she mentioned you,' said Nick, glaring at Clem. 'But she left out the important bit. That you were her twin.' He turned back to Charity. 'I apologise sincerely, Senora Santana, but you must admit the likeness is incredible! To crown it all, I'd even seen the dress before, I was certain you were Clemency.'

'I will ring the doctor,' said Luiz decisively. 'You may have the concussion.'

'I don't need a doctor——' protested Nick.

'It would be better,' chimed in Milagrita. 'How do you do? I am Milagrita Carreras, cousin of Luiz.'

'Nicholas Wood,' he said automatically, trying to smile, then winced as pain knifed through his head.

'Sit down, Nick,' said Clem. 'I've got some ice here for that swelling.'

'And Dr Gonzalez shall check all is well,' insisted Luiz.

'Please—it's quite unnecessary——'

'I'm afraid it is,' interrupted Charity in a stifled voice. All eyes flew to her as she stood with a hand pressed to her midriff. 'Luiz—I have a little pain.'

Clem dumped the bundle of ice in Nick's hand and collided with Luiz as they both dived for Charity.

'*I* will ring the doctor,' said Milagrita firmly. 'In

the meantime, Charity, you will please lie on the sofa and put up your feet.'

The next hour was an experience no one in the *sala* of the Villa Isabel enjoyed. Dr Gonzalez arrived with admirable speed, but even so there was an interval of unadulterated misery before he came, while Luiz held his wife's hands in his in an agony of anxiety, and Charity spent the entire time reassuring him that she was fine, it was only a little tummy-ache, and not to worry so much.

Clem had an ache in her own stomach, but this was no surprise. She and Charity often experienced each other's pain, without any prior knowledge of each other's illness. The day Charity's appendix was removed in Barcelona, Clem had passed out with a knifing pain in her side in Pimlico. Only the actual labour of childbirth had been given to Charity to suffer alone, to Clem's infinite relief.

But, anxious though she was over Charity, Clem was nevertheless burningly conscious of Nick's brooding presence, which was an embarrassment to everyone, himself most of all. She was deeply grateful to Milagrita, who with unobtrusive tact took him out on the patio and plied him with coffee, while Clem stayed by her sister's side, her brain reeling from several forms of shock as she wondered what on earth Nick was doing here in Cabo Feliz. Apart from causing a hell of a lot of trouble, she thought grimly, wishing he'd make himself scarce. On the other hand, he could hardly be blamed for wanting to know the doctor's verdict on Charity in the circumstances.

It proved surprising. Nothing to do with the baby, the doctor said flatly, after examining the patient. Much more likely something the Senora had eaten for lunch. Then suddenly Pilar, the nursemaid, burst in the room in panic.

'*Doña* Caridad, *las niñas*——'

With an exclamation Luiz tore from the room, commanding Charity to stay still, but she ran after him, followed by Dr Gonzalez, who smiled reassuringly at Clem.

'It is possible I am needed upstairs also.'

He was right. The children were crying with stomach pains, and were eventually sick, as was Charity in turn.

'*Gambas*,' said the doctor, returning downstairs.

'Prawns,' explained Milagrita, coming in from the patio.

'You did not eat them, *senorita*?' asked the doctor.

Clemency admitted that she had, and that she did have a little discomfort, but nothing to speak about. 'I thought I was tuned into Charity's pain,' she said, and Milagrita translated to the doctor, who nodded with keen interest.

'Ah, *si—las gemelas*. Such a miracle of nature!' He kissed both women's hands. 'All will be well tomorrow.'

'Doctor, could I trouble you to look at yet another patient?' said Clem. 'A friend of mine is outside on the patio. He had a fall and hurt his head.'

'Tell him to enter, *senorita*. I will examine him.'

But when Clem went outside the patio was deserted. Nick had slipped away when no one was looking.

'He was there with me when we heard the doctor say it was the *gambas* at fault, not the baby, then I rushed in,' said Milagrita in remorse after Dr Gonzalez had left. 'I wish he had stayed so his wound could be examined. He did not look well, Clemency.'

Clem felt too out of sorts, one way and another, to worry about it overmuch. 'I don't even know where he's staying,' she said, wincing as a twinge of pain caught her in the midriff.

Milagrita smiled. 'Ah, but I do, *chica*. While we were talking outside, he told me he had been lucky enough to find a cancellation at the Isabella this afternoon. He must have checked in while Luiz and I were busy elsewhere in the hotel. It must be fate, Clemency, for your lover to chance on a cancellation at this time of the year.'

'He's not my lover.'

'But he was.'

'Exactly, Senora Carreras! Past tense. *Was*.' Clem clutched at her stomach as another cramp seized her. 'And for the moment all I can think of are those wretched *gambas*, not lovers. 'I'm beginning to feel decidedly off myself!'

'Go to bed, *querida*. I shall bring you some hot tea, and the pills the doctor left, and then Luiz and I shall dine alone, I think.' Milagrita's eyes sparkled. 'Such excitement! *Dios*—and to think you came here to Cabo Feliz for a rest!'

CHAPTER SEVEN

AFTER a night when her stomach joined forces with her troubled mind to keep her awake for hours, Clem got up very early, feeling a trifle washed out, but no longer queasy, or in pain. Everyone seemed to be asleep as she stole out of the house and made her way down the path to the small sliver of beach. She wandered along the shore, gazing out to sea at the fishing-boats on the horizon in the pearly morning light. It was surprisingly cool, too cool to swim yet, and she was glad of the fleecy track-suit top she wore over her swimsuit as she sat cross-legged on the pebbles, wondering how Nick was feeling this morning.

Looked at in the cold light of day, the events of the evening before seemed like a scene from a farce. Her holiday had been so peaceful until then, sunlit days on the beach and long evenings spent talking over dinner, then wham! Nicholas Wood materialised out of the dark and there was chaos. It was humiliating to admit she herself was partly to blame. Clem knew very well she should have told Nick she had a twin, but over the years she'd grown very tired of jokes about 'two for the price of one', and 'can your sister's husband tell you apart? In actual fact, Luiz had never had the least difficulty in knowing which twin was which from the very first.

Charity had a small scar on her leg, which was the only real distinguishing mark between them, but Luiz had been immediately aware of other differences: the slight nuances of temperament, a faint variation in the timbre of the voices, the odd mannerism that was peculiar to one twin only.

Nick, if she were fair, had been under a definite disadvantage last night, Clem conceded. Charity had even been wearing a dress he'd already seen in Putney. Not surprising he'd got the wrong end of the stick. Clem kicked moodily at a pebble. She still felt Nick should have known the difference the moment he kissed Charity. Unless Luiz had knocked him down before he had time to recognise it, of course. She got restlessly to her feet and began wandering along the beach again, blind to the beauty of the morning for once as she tried to analyse her feelings on seeing Nick again. Her blood had run ice-cold when she had thought he was dead, admittedly, just as it had after their telephone conversation the night he had told her to stay out of his life. But it had been no time before it had almost boiled with rage when she heard why Luiz had knocked him down.

Clem hugged her arms across her chest. Perhaps she should be flattered that he'd come chasing after her to Spain. Instead she felt embarrassed rather than gratified, because of the uproar which marked his arrival. She heard footsteps on the pebbles and turned, smiling, expecting Luiz. Her smile vanished as she saw Nick advancing towards her. He wore a sweatshirt much like hers, and ancient denim shorts which left most of his long brown legs bare, unlike his eyes, which were hidden behind the lenses of ultra-dark glasses as he stopped a few feet away to look at her.

'Good morning, Clemency.'

'Good morning,' she said tonelessly.

'I saw you from my window, so I came down.'

'I didn't realise this beach was visible from the hotel.'

'I imagine it's only my window that overlooks it. I'm in the belfry room.'

'I see.' Clem looked away out to sea at the sardine fleet. How odd it was, making conversation with a man she'd once made love with so passionately. 'How did you find out where I was?'

Nick moved to stand beside her. 'Emma told me.'

'I particularly asked her not to tell you anything at all, in the unlikely event of your asking any more questions about me.'

'I know. She told me that too. She salved her conscience by persuading herself your whereabouts weren't in the precise category you meant.' Nick traced patterns in the sand with the toe of his canvas shoe. 'I wish she'd told me you had a twin. I wish to God *you* had too, if it comes to that. Long ago.'

'I began to tell you several times,' she said defensively.

'What stopped you?'

'You did. You shut me up very effectively on each occasion, mostly by holding forth about keeping certain areas of one's life private. At other times you stopped my mouth in a different way. By making love to me.' Clem spoke with a detachment she could tell got Nick on the raw.

'I'm glad you can be so objective about it,' he said grimly.

'So am I.'

There was an awkward pause.

'How are your sister and her children this morning?' Nick asked after a while.

'I don't know—they weren't up. But they were a little better late last night. So was I.'

'Were *you* ill too?'

'Only slightly. I thought it was just the usual sympathetic twin stuff. But the prawns were the culprits.'

'My brain got scrambled enough after contact with your brother-in-law's fist, but when I realised your sister might be miscarrying I nearly went off my head,' said Nick grimly.

'Ah yes, I'm forgetting my manners. How *is* your head?'

'Bloody sore. But I'll live.'

'I wouldn't have taken bets on it when I saw you laid out cold on the patio.'

He smiled at her ironically. 'And how did you feel about my apparent demise?'

Clem shrugged. '*I* went rather cold too, for a moment. Then Luiz explained exactly *why* you were out for the count, and I hotted up quickly enough.'

There was an interval of tight-drawn silence while both of them stared out to sea.

'I've already made my apologies to Santana this morning,' Nick said eventually. 'He begins his day early.'

'Luiz works very hard at this time of year.'

There was another tense pause, then Nick turned to face her.

'He was the man I saw, Clemency.'

Her eyes were dispassionate on his bleak face. 'You said something about it last night. What did you mean?'

Nick put out a hand as though he meant to touch her, but she moved back and he dropped it again. 'That weekend, when I was driving down to your place in Wales, I stopped several times along the way to give my eye a rest. Which is how I came to be sitting in the car park of one of the motorway service stations and caught sight of someone I was sure was you. In a car with another man.'

'Ah!' Clem nodded. 'I see. You saw Charity and Luiz.'

'Yes.' He reddened suddenly and turned away. 'He was kissing her, and she was kissing him back. I couldn't look away. I'm not normally a voyeur, but remember I thought it was you. He-he was feeding her chocolates.'

Clem shot a quizzical glance at him. 'Hardly a felony.'

'No.' Nick looked uncomfortable. 'But he put them between his lips and she took them from his with hers.'

'Good heavens!'

He turned on her suddenly and grabbed her

hands. 'That's what sent me so beserk, Clemency—the very fact that there was nothing in the least lewd about the little scene I witnessed. It was the sheer tenderness and intimacy of it that got to me so badly. It was patently obvious that the guy adored her. And worst of all, from my point of view, I could see you—she—adored *him* just as much.'

'She does.'

'Ah, but I thought it was *you*, remember. So I drove out of that service station like a bat out of hell and cleared off to London again.'

Clem's eyes dropped to their clasped hands, her mind in a turmoil. 'I would have explained that same night, but you never gave me a chance.'

'I was roaring drunk, and off my head with jealousy and . . .' He paused, considering his words carefully. 'Disillusion, I think. Because we met in such extraordinary circumstances, I suppose I thought of you as the original fairy off the Christmas tree.'

Clem looked up at him steadily. 'While I'm just ordinary and mortal like everyone else—just as I've always been.'

'Mortal, maybe.' Nick pulled her gently towards him. 'Ordinary, never. I'd never met anyone more beautiful in my life. Until last night, of course. And now I find there are two of you.'

Clem's eyes hardened, and she jerked her hands away. 'Oh no, Nick. There's only one of me. *Me*—Clemency Vaughan. Just as Charity is someone else quite individual too, in spite of the resemblance. It may interest you to know we both met Luiz Santana at exactly the same time when we were nineteen, but only Charity fell in love with him at first sight. I didn't.'

Nick took off his dark glasses to look at her very closely. 'What is it you're trying to say?'

'Last night, after the dust settled, I was in bed with peace to think, and I kept remembering something Luiz once said. It was quite soon after he met Charity. We were on the beach and she showed him the little scar on her leg. It was the only distinguishing mark between us at the time, but he said it was unnecessary. He would know her anywhere, even in the dark.' Clem smiled rather sadly. 'It was dark on the patio last night, wasn't it? So you didn't pass the test. You thought Charity was me, even though you got as far as actually kissing her.'

Nick winced. 'God, what a mess!' He rubbed his eyes wearily and replaced the sunglasses. 'What can I say? I'm sorry, Clemency. Sorry I made such a hell of a scene with your family, that I threw all those insults at you, and most of all that I came chasing after you in Spain. I'd have done a lot better to stay out of your life——'

'As you told me to stay out of yours,' Clem reminded him.

He shrugged. 'I think I was justified at that particular time. How the hell was I to know you had a twin? For God's sake, why didn't you ever *tell* me?'

'I've told you why,' she snapped, then eyed him challengingly. 'So you place the blame for all this squarely on my shoulders, then?'

Nick's mouth tightened. 'If I'd known about Charity, I'd have known who Luiz Santana was, and I'd have introduced myself, then driven on down to your parents' home that evening and asked your father formally for his daughter's hand in the good old-fashioned way.'

Clem stood very still. 'Shouldn't you have asked *me* first?'

'It never even occurred to me that it was necessary. It seemed inevitable from the minute we met. And I could have sworn you felt the same. Do you deny it?'

'No.' Her eyes fell, and she turned away, arms folded.

'Whereas,' Nick went on, 'in actual fact I offended your parents, alienated myself from you, harassed your friends in Putney and last night—last night I made such a fool of myself, I go cold whenever I think of that scene up there.' He jerked his head towards the villa. 'It does nothing for a man's ego to find himself knocked cold by an enraged husband, I assure you. Not to mention the utter horror of the moment when I realised your sister might lose her baby on my account.'

Clem eyed Nick with resentment, incensed at the mere idea of sharing any blame for the incident of the night before. 'If you feel so strongly about it all, I'm surprised you're still here!' she said, and turned to go.

Nick leapt and caught her, pulling her back against him.

'Because I wanted to prove something to myself,' he muttered, and tossed his sunglasses on the sand and kissed her.

With a choked cry Clem fought to push him away, but Nick tightened his hold, his lips forcing hers apart. When he raised his head he was breathing heavily and Clem was scarlet with rage.

'I had to find out for myself,' he panted. 'Last night—last night it was different.'

'It was *Charity*!'

'I know now. This morning it's you. Even unwilling and mad as hell with me, the chemistry still works.' His eyes blazed down at her in triumph.

'So what?' said Clem scornfully. 'There's more to life than chemistry. How about a little trust, a little faith, and some in-depth study of what lies beneath the vital statistics, Nicholas Wood!' Suddenly she tugged the sweatshirt over her head and threw it on the sand, standing erect and proud before him in a brief two-piece swimsuit the exact blue of her eyes. 'Take a good long look. But remember that what you see is merely the cover. Underneath there's the book. The Clemency Vaughan life story—the real me you weren't prepared to study enough to realise there might have been some explanation for what you saw that day.' She saw his eyes dilate at the sight of her almost nude body, and exulted as his teeth clenched and the scar stood out on his face. She smiled in triumph as her eyes travelled deliberately to the place where his tight denim shorts failed to hide his body's response to the sight of her. 'Just as I thought. If I were a bag of bones or had a squint, or whatever, I don't suppose for a minute you'd spare me a second glance. Yet the same me would be underneath.'

'That isn't logical,' he said harshly.

'Maybe not.' Clem pulled the sweatshirt on again, and ran a hand through her untidy hair. 'Look, Nick, you hurt me so much I thought I'd die. Then after a while I realised one doesn't die. One gets on with life and recovers bit by bit, and takes damn good care not to expose oneself to the precise form of hurt that caused the wound in the first place.'

'You're fortunate to possess such facile powers of recovery!'

'Facile?' She breathed in deeply, her eyes glittering. 'You just proved my point. You don't know the real me at all.' She held his gaze for a few deliberate moments, then said coldly, 'Goodbye, Nick. I'd rather we never met again.'

His eyes flickered, then went blank. 'You mean that?'

Clem nodded. 'To use a well-known quote, just stay out of my life.'

He smiled slowly, his face saturnine with mockery. 'I suppose you feel better for saying that. Did it fulfil a deep female need for retaliation?'

Clem seethed, but kept her face blank. 'Do you know, it did, rather.' She looked at her watch. 'It's late, I'd better get back to the house. Goodbye.'

She gave him a cool little nod, then turned on her heel and left him, forcing herself to walk slowly, ignoring the urge to take to her heels and run like the wind. All the way up to the villa she could feel Nick's eyes trained on her back, and as she reached the sanctuary of the patio a quick glance towards the beach confirmed he was still standing where she'd left him, watching her as she disappeared into the house.

The little maid told her Charity was still in bed, but Dolly and Luiza were lying together on the sofa, their little gold-skinned faces brightening as their aunt appeared.

'Mama's sick,' announced Dolly, 'and Luiza and me were sick too.'

'*Me duele aquí*,' said Luiza, rubbing her small stomach dolefully.

'Oh, darlings, what a shame!' Clem hugged both little girls, then promised to play with them after she'd visited their mother.

Charity looked ghastly. Beads of perspiration ran down her colourless face.

'My God!' exclaimed Clem in alarm. 'Are you still being sick?'

'Yes. I'm sick some mornings anyway, love. Goes with the condition.' She smiled gamely. 'Just don't ever mention prawns again. Are you all right?'

'Yes. But then, I didn't eat as much as you, piggy!'

'Don't rub it in. Did you have any dinner last night?'

'No.' Clem sat down on the bed and smoothed the damp curls back from her sister's forehead. 'I've just been down on the beach. I was up early this morning. So was Nick.'

Charity brightened and sat up slowly, taking a few experimental deep breaths as Clem pushed pillows behind her. 'Thanks. I'm winning, I think. Did you talk?'

'Yes.' Clem gave her sister a rough outline of the exchange. 'What it boils down to, it seems, is that it's all my fault for not telling him I had a twin.'

Charity thought this over. 'I suppose he's right in a way. It would have saved a lot of trouble if you had, if one's honest.' She eyed Clem searchingly. 'Tell me the truth—have you always minded being a twin?'

'Good God, no!' Clem bent quickly to kiss her sister's wan cheek. 'Surely you know that, muggins. Apart from the bond, to be schmaltzy, it was always such fun. I used to pity girls who didn't have a twin. We were always a great double act, Chatty, particularly in college.' She paused, choosing her words with care, as she went on to explain that things had changed after that. Because Charity had met Luiz when she was still very young, and married him as soon as she left college, the situation had altered dramatically. When Charity had left to marry Luiz, she went a long way out of Clem's life, not only because she went to live in Spain, but because she had a husband for her other half instead of her twin.

For the first time Clem told Charity about her own feelings at the time, that with no immediate job in view she'd felt vulnerable and alone and, however much she dismissed it as nonsense, lacking

n some way no one seemed able to help, not even
heir parents, who were aware of their child's
problem, but were helpless to solve it. Which was
vhy she'd moved in with Evan Rees. His warmth
nd casual friendliness were oddly comforting and,
ecause he'd known the Vaughan girls all the way
hrough college, he took Clem's looks for granted.
Best of all, he knew she was a twin. With other men
he had come to detest the inevitable reaction and
omments when she confessed she had a double.

Charity looked troubled as Clem came to a halt.
And I always thought I knew everything about
ou,' she said soberly. 'I never dreamed you felt
leserted.'

'But I didn't really. No one was happier for you
han me, Chatty. It's just that I'd never made any
lose friends because I always had you, I suppose,
nd suddenly there I was on my own. Kit was
narried, so were you, and I didn't want to stay at
ome, so I took Evan up on his offer for the sake of
ompany as much as anything else.'

'And look where that got you!'

Clem nodded soberly. 'I hit a real low after he
vas killed. Thank God I bumped into Robina that
lay. I was so lucky to have someone ask me to work
t something I enjoy so much. And then I was
ucky to have girls like Emma and Jane answer my
dvertisement for someone to share the house.
They've been very good to me. Robina has too,
ecause she insists I go to those upmarket thrashes
f hers sometimes. I met Hugo at one of those,
ctually, so I suppose in a way it was through

Robina that I eventually met Nick.'

'Yes, Nick. What happens about him now?'

'A few minutes ago I told him to get lost.'

Charity groaned. 'You nitwit!'

'Not at all,' said Clem airily. 'My mistake was in thinking he was my knight in shining armour. He fell of his charger with a clang, as far as I'm concerned. He should have known you weren't me.'

'How?'

'I don't know. He just should have!' Clem changed the subject quickly. 'By the way, do you make a habit of sharing sweeties with Luiz in a rather peculiar way?'

Charity flushed bright red. 'How do you know that?'

'Because that's what Nick witnessed so inopportunely in a motorway service station; you and your husband doing erotic things with chocolate creams!'

'I think I'm going to be sick again——'

'Oh no, you don't. Drink this.' Clem thrust a glass of mineral water at her sister and Charity gulped it down hurriedly, then lay back, looking slightly better.

'Go and tell him you're sorry, Clem,' she coaxed.

'No.'

'I felt very sorry for him last night. Besides,' Charity smiled naughtily, 'he's a world-class kisser, Clem. Almost as good as Luiz.'

Clem rose to her feet with dignity. 'I am now going downstairs to see to your daughters, Senora Santana. And you'd better stay where you are until lunchtime, if you know what's good for you.'

'But I'll be bored!' wailed Charity.

'If you don't, I shall tell that jealous Latin husband of yours exactly what you said about Nick's kisses.'

'You wouldn't!'

'No?' Laughing, Clem left her sister to rest, and went downstairs to make herself some breakfast. She persuaded Dolly and Luiza to share her toast, then spent the morning with them, keeping them entertained on the shady patio with puzzles and games until they were back to normal.

Luiz hurried in to visit his wife and daughters at one stage, and later on Milagrita came for coffee, agog with curiosity to know if Clem had seen Nick. Clem admitted she had, and given him his marching orders.

'Do you know if he's left yet?' she added casually.

'I do not think so,' said Milagrita. 'Do you really want him to go away, *querida*?'

By this time Clem had long since lost the glow of satisfaction from serving Nick with his own medicine.

'I think maybe *I'll* go,' she said listlessly. 'If Nick decides to stay on, it might be best if I just went back to work.'

Milagrita nobly refrained from comment, merely patting Clem's shoulder in sympathy as she got up. 'I shall run upstairs and see how Charity feels. Meanwhile you will keep an eye on our *sobrinas*, and do nothing rash, I beg.'

When she came downstairs later, Milagrita looked

worried. 'I do not think Charity feels well at all, Clemency. Perhaps it might be best if she, how do you say, takes it easy for a while.'

Clem jumped up in alarm. 'I'll go up and see if she needs anything.'

'*Bueno*. I will have my lunch here with you and *las niñas* today.' Milagrita smiled at her delighted nieces, and swept them off to the kitchen to tell Pilar what they fancied.

'Are you all right?' demanded Clem, as she hurried into Charity's bedroom.

'I'm OK,' said Charity faintly. 'Just a bit off, that's all.'

'All that brouhaha last night knocked you for six,' said Clem bitterly.

'No, it didn't. It was the prawns.' Charity looked up at her sister coaxingly. 'Why don't you go out this afternoon? I'm going to have a long sleep, and Milagrita says she can be spared from the hotel for a while to stay with the girls. There's a market today in the village, with loads of things you could take back to Putney for presents.'

Clem looked doubtful. 'I was thinking about going home right away, actually.'

Tears welled up in Charity's blue eyes. 'Oh, please don't go yet, Clem. Wait till I feel better.' She sniffed hard. 'We don't see each other that much—it'll probably be ages before you get away again.'

Clem sighed, defeated. 'All right, don't get upset. I'll stay a bit longer.'

'And you will take a break this afternoon?'

'Since you're so set on it, I suppose so.'

Once Clem was satisfied Charity was settled comfortably, she went downstairs to rejoin Milagrita for lunch with the children. Afterwards Milagrita went back to the hotel for an hour to relieve the receptionist on duty, promising to return to look after Dolly and Luiza while Clem went out for a while. Once the little girls were sleeping Clem stood for a time under the shower, then put on a thin cotton dress and flat sandals to go exploring the delights of the *mercado* in the village. As usual she tied a scarf over her hair and wore a large straw hat to avoid the embarrassment of being mistaken for Senora Santana, and, armed with sunglasses, camera and purse, left Pilar temporarily in charge and went off to climb the steep road to the village.

Cabo Feliz was just coming to life after its siesta as Clem wandered along the narrow road which detoured the village and took her to the market without going past the Hotel Isabella. The village sported a craft shop. The small whitewashed building with *Artesania* blazoned above the door had woven straw objects of all kinds hanging outside on its walls: great circular hats, baskets, rugs, and a row of horned straw bull heads as a finishing touch. The produce and foodstuffs of the morning had long gone from the small square, but there were souvenirs of every kind in the remaining stalls: brass, wrought iron, leather, ceramics, rugs of the type Clem had seen in Granada, paintings of varied artistry and appeal. Vendors accosted Clem, protesting the quality of their wares, and she smiled and shook her head and wandered slowly among the goods on display, searching for something to take back for Emma and Jane.

A fringed rug caught her eye, and she gestured to the vendor to spread it out. She stood back to admire its surprisingly muted colours, deciding it would suit the parlour in Putney admirably.

'*Cuánto es?*' she asked, and the smiling man named a price Clem converted quickly into sterling. She felt sure he was taking advantage of the lone lady tourist, and smiled back at him, shaking her head, and he promptly lowered the price a little. Sorrowfully she shook her head again, and so it went on until a price had been reached agreeable to both and somewhere more in keeping with the rug's worth.

As she received the package, Clem was startled by a voice in her ear asking her if she needed help. She forced herself to breathe normally, and turned to confront Nick, who looked cool in cricket shirt and faded denims as he watched the proceedings with interest.

'I can manage,' she said stiffly, glad of the dark lenses that hid the flare of delight in her eyes at the sight of him.

'I'm sure you can,' he said cheerfully, but relieved her of the rug, and stayed by her side as she went on with her souvenir hunt.

'I thought you'd have gone by now,' Clem remarked, as she feigned deep interest in the paintings on display.

'Did you?' He pointed at a small canvas. 'That's

good. It's the cove below your sister's villa.'

Clem examined the picture, secretly charmed by the impression of heat the artist put across with ochre sand and bone-white pebbles against a dark green backdrop of umbrella pines.

'Do you like it?' asked Nick.

'Rather nice,' she admitted, resisting the temptation to say 'no' just because he'd been clever enough to spot it.

'Shall I haggle?' Nick peered under the hat brim in enquiry.

'If you like.'

To Clem's surprise, he turned a flood of fluent Catalan-flavoured Spanish on the man offering the picture, and a goodnatured wrangle ensued, enjoyed by everyone around, as Nick beat the man down to what he considered reasonable for the painting.

'Let me make you a present of it, Clemency,' he said afterwards, waving her proffered money aside. 'Please. As something to remember me by.'

Her smile was ironic as she accepted. 'I don't imagine I'll need anything to remind me of you, Nick, ever, one way and another. But I like the picture very much. Thank you.'

They looked at each other steadily for a few moments in silence, then, as if some kind of truce had been tacitly agreed, they wandered on together to browse through the rest of the goods on show.

'Do you mean to do all your shopping today?' asked Nick eventually.

'It seemed a good idea. I'm not staying long—just

until Charity's better.'

Nick looked at her sharply. 'Your sister's ill?'

'No more, I'm assured, than a combination of prawns and pregnancy can be expected to make her feel.' Clem smiled reassuringly. 'Don't worry—she's in no danger of losing the baby. Though more by luck than good management after the alarums and excursions of last night.'

Nick turned his attention to an Arab-style carved chess set. 'I'm likely to get nightmares about last night for a long, long time. Every time I think of what I did, I want to beat *myself* over the head!'

'Better than wanting to beat *me* over the head!'

'My mother brought me up never to hit girls.'

'Very commendable. Does your head still hurt a lot?'

'Not nearly as much as my heart.' Nick fixed her with a grave, unsmiling look, then turned away to point out a hand-carved wooden bowl. 'That's genuinely old, unless I'm mistaken. Want me to do my stuff?'

Clem nodded mutely, unable to trust her voice for the moment. Nick's voice had been so casual, she could hardly believe he'd meant what he said. Yet his look had underlined his words—and left her feeling breathless as she stood very still while her heartbeat returned to normal, her eyes very thoughtful on Nick's laughing face as he bargained for the bowl.

'I should go back now,' she said, when the transaction was completed to the satisfaction of all concerned.

'I'll carry your loot for you.'

Clem thought of refusing, then changed her mind and smiled politely instead. 'Thank you. Just leave it at the hotel reception desk, then Luiz can bring it down to the villa later.'

Nick eyed her warily. 'Unless you violently object, I'd like to walk back to the villa with you. I'm anxious to make my apologies to your sister.'

Clem shrugged. 'If you must.'

His smile grew sardonic. 'Thank you.'

They talked desultorily on neutral subjects as they walked together through the village and began the descent through the pines to the Villa Isabel, both of them avoiding further references to anything remotely personal. When they arrived at the house, the scene they interrupted was idyllic. Charity lay on a sunbed on the patio, a daughter in the crook of each arm, while Dolly and Luiza turned the pages of the book their mother was reading to them.

'Mr Wood!' said Charity with a delighted smile. 'How very nice. Come and have some tea.'

Nick took the hand she held up to him and kissed it gravely, taking off his sunglasses as he smiled at the little girls. 'Senora Santana——'

'Charity, please,' she said, smiling mischievously, 'since for obvious reasons my face must look very familiar to you. Besides, after last night I feel we need no introduction.'

To Clem's surprise, colour rose along Nick's sharp cheekbones. 'Which brings me straight to why I came back with Clemency. I've come to apologise humbly for behaving like a barbarian last night.'

Charity laughed, and glanced towards Clem, who was busily divesting herself of hat and scarf. 'I accept wholeheartedly, Nick, because I'll tell you frankly, I don't feel you were wholly to blame. Clem should have told you she had a double.'

'I don't suppose it would have made much difference if she had. I'd never have believed her.' His smile was rueful. 'I thought Clemency was one of a kind.'

'I am,' murmured Clem.

Nick ignored her. 'Nothing on earth would have convinced me anyone else could be as beautiful.'

Clem gave him a hostile look, then beckoned to the little girls. 'Say how do you do to Mr Wood, my lovelies, then let's go and make tea for Mama.'

Nick squatted on his heels to kiss each small, dimpled hand, telling the children how pleased he was to make their acquaintance, first in English, then in Spanish, to their delight, after which Clem was obliged to make tea alone, because neither Dolly nor Luiza would budge from the fascinating stranger's side. While Clem was loading a tray, Charity came to help.

'Where did you meet him?' she whispered, as she arranged biscuits on a plate.

'Near Artesania.' Clem kept her eyes on the teapot she was filling with boiling water.

'Have you made it up?'

'No.'

'He wants to, Clem.'

Clem shrugged, and Charity scowled at her.

'And *you* want to really, too. Don't you?'

'No.' Clem lifted the tray.

'Who are you trying to kid, Clemency Vaughan? This is *me*. I tune in to your frequency, remember? You want him all right.'

'I didn't say I didn't.' Clem met her twin's eyes, resigned. 'But I'm not at all sure I want to start anything up again. Far too painful when it ends.'

'Must it end?'

'What guarantee do I have that it won't? It did once.' Clem went on out to the patio before Charity could say any more on the subject.

Milagrita joined the tea-party shortly afterwards, her silvery Santana eyes gleaming with curiosity when she found that not only was Nicholas Wood one of the group, but that her nieces were enthroned on his lap, involved in deep discussion about the scar on his face. After a flurry of introductions, it was only a short while before Milagrita showed signs of being just as much taken with the visitor as Charity and the little girls, and after a while Clem excused herself on the pretext of taking her spoils up to her room, thoroughly irritated by Nick's instant success with every female, young and old, who laid eyes on him.

Like a pasha with his harem, she thought crossly, as she lingered alone in her room, knowing full well it was childish to feel annoyed, because Nick's charm had the same effect on others as herself. *Had* being the correct tense, she told herself acidly, and took time over brushing her hair and putting on lipstick. When she rejoined the others, Nick deposited Dolly and Luiza gently on their feet and stood up, hastily resuming the protection of his sunglasses.

'I've just been asking your sister if I could steal you away for an evening,' he said quietly. 'I'd very much like to take you out to dinner.'

Charity nodded vigorously behind his back, her eyes signalling messages to Clem.

'Lovely idea,' she said firmly. 'Clem hasn't been out in the evening since she arrived. She could do with a bit of nightlife.'

Clem frowned at her. 'I'm perfectly happy here at the villa, Chatty. I came for a rest, remember. My aim was peace—and privacy,' she added deliberately, looking at Nick.

'I'll be leaving soon,' he said, unruffled. 'I'm staring a new job.'

'Leaving television?'

'Yes, as a matter of fact. Why not drive to S'Agaro with me later? I'll tell you all about it.'

Milagrita joined in the surreptitious gestures of encouragement and Clem smiled involuntarily, which Nick took for consent.

'Thank you, Clem,' he said quietly. 'I'll call for you at eight, if that's all right.'

'Not tonight,' she said quickly, ignoring Charity's dagger-like glare. 'I still feel a bit washed out after yesterday.'

'Then perhaps tomorrow night?' said Nick doggedly.

In the face of so much opposition Clem couldn't bring herself to refuse a second time, and she nodded, resigned. 'Very well—tomorrow night. I'll look forward to it,' she added, and flushed, as Charity's knowing smile showed she knew very well that her sister's polite little sentence was more in the nature of the simple truth than a meaningless courtesy.

CHAPTER EIGHT

HAVING refused Nick's invitation to dinner, Clem found the evening dragged surprisingly, and was glad, for the first time ever in Spain, when it was time to go to bed.

'Mother would say you'd cut off your nose to spite your face,' observed Charity, when Clem's restlessness grew so obvious even Luiz noticed it.

'What does that mean, *mi corazón?*' he asked his wife.

'That Clem really wanted very much to have dinner with Nick Wood tonight, but was too bloody-minded to say yes straight off.'

'Ah, I see.' Luiz smiled at his flushed sister-in-law. 'Your pride would not allow you to consent without a little resistance, Clem. You want to make this Nick suffer.'

Clem shrugged. 'Not at all. I just felt tired.'

'Which is why you're driving us crazy by jumping up every five minutes looking for something to do,' Charity grinned knowingly.

'If I'm being such a nuisance, I might as well go to bed,' said Clem with dignity, but smiled sheepishly as Charity hugged her when she said goodnight.

Luiz kissed Clem's cheek, then took her hand and looked at her very soberly. 'I like this man of yours, Clemency, even though I wished to murder him at first. I have sympathy with him. If Charity had not returned my love, life would have been meaningless for me.'

Clem stared at him in surprise, not a little embarrassed by such a dramatic statement. 'Why, Luiz——'

'In other words,' said Charity, with a luminous look at her husband, 'why keep Nick on tenterhooks when it's as plain as the nose on your face the man's bananas over you?'

'It may be to you. Personally, I'm not convinced.' Clem smiled at them both and went off to bed, rather shaken just the same. Luiz was an unexpected champion for Nick, in the circumstances.

To her surprise Clem slept well, and was up early with the children, insisting Charity stayed in bed until mid-morning. When breakfast was over Clem bundled a few necessary belongings into her beach bag, took Dolly and Luiza by the hand and went off down to the beach to play with them on the sand before the sun grew too hot. They ran about with a large ball for a while, then splashed about in the sea for a few minutes, while Clem encouraged her small nieces' efforts at swimming, then she took them back to the sunbeds for a rest. The three of them were enjoying mugs of cold orange juice from the insulated jug Clem produced from her bag, when footsteps crunched behind them on the pebbles, and Dolly and Luiza jumped up in excitement to greet the stranger they had taken to with such enthusiasm the day before.

In the face of such a vociferous welcome from her

nieces, Clem had no option but to smile politely at Nick, and ask him to join them.

'Are you feeling better this morning?' he asked.

'Much better. Sit down and have some orange juice.'

Nick did as she said with flattering alacrity, the wary look fading from his face as he sat on the other sunbed with a small girl close on either side of him.

'Actually I slept like a log last night,' she said. 'How about you?'

'I can't say the same, exactly.' He gave her an unsettling look. 'I seem to have lost the habit of sleep since I met you, Clemency. In the short time you were with me it seemed a waste of precious time, and since then I've been too bloody miserable to sleep much at all.'

Clem felt the colour rushing to her face, and turned away to pick up the shirt she'd worn to walk down from the villa. Suddenly she seemed in need of protective covering, and thanked Nick breathlessly as he bent forward to help her on with the shirt.

'Can you do puzzles?' demanded Dolly, and Nick blinked, then smiled at the small girl at his knee, assuring her he was an expert. The tense moment passed as Clem helped the children unpack the supply of books and puzzles they insisted on taking with them everywhere.

It was oddly enjoyable to sit under the big umbrella with Nick and the children, especially after they tired of their jigsaws and demanded a story. Clem lay back, listening to the deep, articulate voice telling an updated version of Goldilocks and the

Three Bears, her eyes dreamy as she watched the relaxed dark man holding her nieces in thrall, thinking what a good father he'd make. Her mind skidded to a stop. The thought of Nick as a father took her breath away. Because suddenly it was crystal clear to her that, if Nicholas Wood had any intention of fathering children, she very definitely wanted to be their mother.

When the tale was finished, the little girls looked up beseechingly at Nick.

'Do you know more stories?' asked Dolly eagerly, always the spokeswoman for the two children.

Nick admitted he did, then looked across at Clem very deliberately. 'I know a very beautiful story about Cinderella, but I can't tell it yet, sweetheart, because I'm not sure of the ending.'

Clem gazed back at him dumbly, unable to tear her eyes away from the sudden heated intensity in his.

The intrusion of Pilar was a welcome relief from the flood of emotion threatening to overwhelm her. Charity, it seemed, had coffee ready at the villa, and would be pleased if the *señor* would accompany the *señorita* and the *niñas* to the house to join her. Nick accepted without hesitation, and took Dolly and Luiza by the hand as he walked up the beach with Clem. She was very conscious of the picture they made as they went up to the house: tall, dark man and tanned, fair woman, the children resembling the latter enough to make them seem like a family. And Clem knew very well the same thought was in Charity's mind when her sister gave a warm welcome to the visitor. Her penetrating blue eyes had a habit of homing in on her twin's thoughts far too easily for Clem's peace of mind.

'You haven't changed your mind, Clemency?' said Nick, as he rose to go later. She looked at him blankly. 'About driving to S'Agaro tonight,' he added quickly.

'No, I'm looking forward to it,' she said candidly, and was rewarded by a smile of such warmth from Nick that her colour surged up under her tan in response.

'Thank you——' He made an involuntary move towards her, then checked himself quickly. He turned to Charity and the little girls to say goodbye, then looked back at Clem. 'Will eight o'clock suit you?'

She nodded, smiling, and returned his wave as he went away.

Clem had never been to S'Agaro, which Charity warned her was considered the cream of the coastal resorts, and merited something dressy if Nick was taking her out for an expensive dinner.

'I don't know that a pricey meal is what he has in mind.'

'He is taking you to the Hotel de la Gavina,' said Luiz, who had joined them for lunch. 'He asked me to advise him earlier,' he informed them smugly.

'Did he now?' said Charity, greatly impressed.

Clem's eyebrows rose. 'Is it a very smart place?'

Luiz nodded. 'The most luxurious hotel in these parts, *chica*.'

Charity kissed her husband and jumped to her feet. 'Then you'll need to borrow a dress, Clem. I don't suppose you've brought anything formal.'

'Formal?' protested Clem as she was dragged upstairs. 'I'm on holiday, Chatty. Surely my black dress will do?'

'No. You'd better wear the white one you made for me. I can't for the moment, it's too tight.'

'But it's not my style,' protested Clem, whose taste was different from her twin's when it came to clothes. Her own tendency was to minimise her curves, whereas Charity made no bones about emphasising the assets given her by nature.

Clem's protests were useless. Charity brushed them aside ruthlessly, and when Clem finally went downstairs that evening, shortly before Nick was due, she wore a clinging white silk sheath whose exquisite cut was its only ornament, apart from a cluster of green-stemmed silk lilies of the valley Clem had made to wear on one shoulder.

Luiz rolled his eyes and kissed her hand. 'The miracles God is able to perform! Almost I believe you are Charity.'

'Well, she's not,' said his wife, pulling him away. 'So hands off, *mi marido*.'

'Tell me where I may put my hands instead,' he said promptly, kissing her, and Clem protested loudly.

'Do me a favour, you two. Wait until I'm gone, at least!'

Nick arrived promptly, formally dressed in lightweight suit and white shirt with a dark tie. As he accepted a drink from Luiz, Charity caught Clem's eyes in triumph, with no need for the unspoken 'I told you so' as her glance flicked up and down the white silk dress. After a pleasant interval Nick smiled regretfully and said it was time to go if they were to be in time for dinner in S'Agaro, and ushered Clem outside to the small open area on the cliff-top where he'd parked the Mini hired for his stay.

'Is it far to S'Agaro?' she asked as they set off.

'Only a few kilometres. I booked dinner for nine.' Nick's voice sounded a little weary, and she stole a look at him, wondering if something were wrong.

'Is your head still aching?' she asked.

'No.' He smiled at her briefly as they left the village. 'Otherwise I wouldn't attempt this coast road, which is undeniably beautiful, but makes for tricky driving with all the doubling back around the inlets in the cliffs.'

Nick was right. The route was scenic, but demanded full concentration from the driver, and Clem made no attempt at conversation until they arrived in S'Agaro itself, where the palatial setting of the Hotel de la Gavina among its tree-shaded lawns was so impressive, Clem was gladder than ever of the dress and the silk sandals Charity had been adamant on lending her to go with it.

'You look absolutely dazzling tonight,' commented Nick when they were sitting over pre-dinner drinks. The look in his eyes was eloquent. 'That dress is superb.'

'It's Charity's,' said Clem, shrugging. 'She spurned all mine as unworthy of this.' She waved a hand at her surroundings.

Nick leaned back in his chair. 'By which I gather you think I've brought you here to impress.'

Her eyes opened in surprise. 'No, I don't. I can't have been *that* mistaken about you,' she said rashly, then bit her lip, annoyed with her unguarded tongue.

He smiled. 'Actually it's by way of a celebration. Maybe you've forgotten, but I've got a new job.'

Clem had not forgotten. She'd been wondering about it ever since he'd mentioned it.

'I'm leaving television to do a current affairs programme on radio.' He studied her closely as he spoke, as if gauging her reaction.

'Sounds safer, at least. Fewer bullets in a broadcasting studio, for a start.'

'True. It means I also stay in one place for a change.' He looked up impatiently as the waiter arrived with more drinks. Clem smiled her thanks as she accepted hers, which was her favourite Andaluza, a mixture of dry sherry and orange juice, served with soda and shaved ice.

'Good thing Dad isn't here to see my treatment of good Spanish sherry,' she commented.

Nick grinned. 'Not a drink for the purist, but if you like it, why not?'

Clem raised her glass. 'Exactly. Here's to your new job then, Nick. Every success.'

'It's a double celebration, actually.' He took a swallow of his gin and tonic. 'The first half of my book met with surprisingly warm approval from the publishers, so I'm finishing the rest of it at top speed before I start on the new job.'

'Congratulations!' Clem's eyes glowed. 'That'
terrific news, Nick!'

His dark eyes lit with sudden heat, and he leaned
closer to take her hand. 'Clemency——' He broke off
with a stifled curse as menus were placed in front of
them.

The moment passed as they began a discussion of
what to eat, Clem frank about feeling hungry.

'I haven't eaten much since those famous prawns.'

'Choose anything you like,' he said, amused. 'If
that dress will let you.'

'Do you think it's too tight?'

'Only as far as my blood pressure's concerned,' he
said without expression, and applied himself to the
complications of the menu.

Clem expressed a yen for something ethnic. 'Not
too adventurous, though.'

With the waiter's help she chose *jamón serrano*,
red mountain ham sliced so thinly it was translucent,
served with ice-cooled melon. 'And at the risk of
sounding like a tourist,' she said, smiling up at the
waiter, 'I would really love a *paella*.'

'From the dazed look on the poor chap's face, I
think he'd have probably tried to bring you the
moon and stars as garnish, if you'd asked,' said Nick
drily afterwards, his smile rather twisted as she
turned innocent blue eyes on him.

'Sweet, wasn't he?' she said blithely. 'What was he
saying about the *paella*?'

'Merely reminding me that it was prepared in the
Catalan style, without chicken, as is considered
proper in these parts. I also told him easy on the

garlic, as Catalans tend to be rather liberal with it unless curbed.'

'How come you speak such good Spanish?' Clem asked curiously.

'I suppose I possess what's popularly known as an ear for languages. Useful in my line. But I confess I used to come to this part of Spain as a child every summer. My parents loved the area. There were only about a dozen hotels along this coast then. It was a magic sort of place to me. I used to hang out with local fishermen's kids—you could hardly tell me apart from them once I'd been here a day or two, and I just sort of mopped up the language osmosis-fashion.'

'While I, on the other hand, never managed to get to Spain at all until I was nineteen or so. Late developer!' Clem smiled. 'Actually it was a fairly momentous holiday. Practically the moment we arrived, my sisters met the men they're now married to.'

'Didn't anyone take *your* fancy?'

She shook her head. 'No, nary a one.'

'Don't try to tell me it was lack of male interest!' Nick took a look around him. 'Every man in this room envies me my companion, for a start.'

'*Muy guapa!*' said Clem, unimpressed. '*La rubia Inglesa.*'

'Ah! You've heard it all before.'

'Blondes go down well in Latin countries.'

'You sound as though the term "blonde" doesn't please you much.'

'Only because "dumb" tends to get bracketed

with it.' Clem looked up with a sudden dazzling smile as the waiter returned to escort them to their table in the Candlelight Room. The attractive young Spaniard almost fell over himself in his efforts to hold her chair for her, then flicked open the linen napkin for her with panache.

'You see?' murmured Clem, as she began on her delicious cured ham. 'Easy as pie, isn't it?'

'Do I get the feeling you're trying to make a point?' Nick raised his glass of champagne in silent toast.

'Merely that every man you imagine is—is fancying me is after this.' She flicked a finger at her face, then down at her silk-covered breasts. 'The body. Not one of them cares a damn about the fact that I think and hold an intelligent conversation, earn my own living. Mind you, the last would probably meet with approval because sewing is such a *feminine* occupation, isn't it? Highly suitable for a "damn fine woman" like me.'

'Some men have really trodden on your toes, haven't they?' said Nick, whistling. 'Do you lump me in with the rest, Clemency?'

'No. I honestly believed you were different.' She raised probing blue eyes to his. 'I thought you'd seen through the wrappings to the real me inside, otherwise I'd never have let you through my front door, Mr Wood, let alone into my bed.'

He returned the look steadily. 'Where it's just possible I'd still be welcome if you'd ever said the one key word to the whole mix-up. What's so bad about being a twin?'

'Very little.' Clem looked at him thoughtfully, then decided to tell him the story of a young solicitor she'd seen quite a lot of at one time. 'He was someone I liked, fun to be with, and we got on really well. I genuinely believed we had a lot in common. So after a while I told him I had a twin, who was an exact mirror image of myself. He said nothing very much at first, except for the usual surprise. Then eventually he confessed he was tormented by a fantasy which kept him awake at night, maddening him, about having two girls like me in his bed, making love to him at the same time.'

Nick's eyebrows shot into his hair as he glared at her. 'Are you telling me you imagined I was similarly inclined?'

'No, no. I'm just trying to explain why it was so difficult to say I had a twin. At first, anyway. Then afterwards, each time I tried to bring it up . . .'

'I shut you up by making love to you.'

The arrival of the *paella* provided a welcome interruption, after which further conversation was confined to comments on the food for a while, as Clem began on her portion with an appetite she was pleased to find quite unimpaired by her reluctant revelations.

Afterwards, when dessert had been refused in favour of *café solo* and a *coñac*, Nick asked if Clem felt like a walk.

'Or aren't those shoes up to it?' he asked, as they left the hotel.

'Certainly they are!' The night was so beautiful, Clem had no wish to return so early, and agreed readily when Nick proposed walking along the tamarisk-lined belvedere, which led past numbers of inlets on its way to the beach of Sa Conca. Clem was very much intrigued by the oddly dated atmosphere of the resort, with its smattering of elegant houses and beach huts, unsurprised when Nick told her the place dated from the twenties, the design of a Barcelona businessman.

'The Hostal de la Gavina,' he said, as they strolled away from it, 'is still in the hands of the family who built it in the early thirties.'

'It was quite an experience.' Clem looked up at him with a smile. 'Thank you for bringing me, Nick.'

'The pleasure, believe me, was all mine!'

At the note in his voice she turned away hurriedly, and began to talk about the various expeditions she'd made with the obliging Pepe.

'And just who might Pepe be?' asked Nick.

'The son of the maître d' at the Isabella.' Clem gave him a sardonic look. 'All of nineteen years old, and very keen to earn some pocket money while he subjects me to as much religious architecture as he can possibly pack into the space of a couple of hours each afternoon.'

Nick laughed rather sheepishly, and entered into a discussion on the things she'd seen, until without realising it they found they were at the end of the belvedere.

'Sorry, Clem.' Nick smiled down at her ruefully, as they lingered to look at the moonlight silvering the sea of the beautiful Sa Conca beach. 'Are your feet hurting?'

'Really,' she said mockingly. 'All this ravishing scenery spread out in front of you, Nick Wood, and all you can think of is aching feet?'

'By no means.' He pushed his hair back from his face and stared out to sea. 'But it seemed the least inflammatory of the various subjects I *could* put up for discussion.'

There was silence for a while.

'That moon's up there again,' said Clem at last, finding the quiet oppressive.

Nick glanced down at her. 'Are you a moon child, Clemency? Born under the sign of Cancer?'

She shook her head, grinning. 'No fear. My sign is Gemini, of course—the heavenly twins!'

He joined in her laughter, sobering at last as he gazed down into her eyes, oblivious of passers-by. 'You look like a moon child to me. In that dress, in this light, you're almost unreal,' he said huskily.

'Believe me, I'm not, Nick. I'm exactly the same girl you knew in Putney in the rain.'

Their eyes locked for several tense moments, then very carefully Nick took her hand in his as they began the walk back past the tamarisks to the car. Neither seemed willing or able to break the silence between them as they strolled slowly along the belvedere, the way back seeming far longer than the couple of miles Clem knew it must actually be. As they walked in apparent outer harmony, she knew only too well that Nick was as burningly conscious as herself of the simple contact of their hands, of the fingers which formed a junction for the currents of heat and longing that coursed through their veins, as powerful as though they were joined in the ultimate intimacy of love.

Clem felt utterly drained by the time they reached the Mini, and a swift glance at him showed plainly that Nick felt the same. He thrust a hand wearily through his hair as he opened the door for her, and she eyed him closely.

'It may be the moonlight, but you look pretty ghastly to me all of a sudden. What's the matter, Nick?'

'Headache. I get them now and then since this.' He touched a hand to his eye and smiled crookedly. 'Contact with Luiz's fist and the patio floor haven't exactly helped lately, either. I'm determined to lead a quieter life from now on.'

Clem studied his face anxiously in silence, thinking hard. Finally she came to a decision and held out her hand. 'Give me the keys. I'll drive back.'

'I didn't know you could.'

'There's a lot about me you don't know!'

'I'd give my soul for the chance to learn, Clemency!' he muttered thickly.

She pushed him into the passenger seat, very worried by the fact that he offered no argument. Since it was obvious he was feeling far worse than he let on, she slid into the driving seat, took a few minutes to study the details of the unfamiliar right-hand drive, then switched on the ignition and cautiously nosed the car out into the traffic.

'This will probably be a very slow journey,' she warned. 'And don't doze off, please. I'll need instructions. I've never driven on the right-hand side of the road before.'

'Now she tells me!'

'You said you wanted to learn everything about me,' she reminded him.

'Careful! You're a bit near the edge!' Nick sat rigid, staring ahead at the moonlit road.

'Look—do you want to drive?' she demanded irritably.

'Can't. Eye's gone.'

'Gone where?'

'Vision goes in the bad one with migraine—God! You're too close to that car!'

After a while Clem got more into the rhythm of things, growing used to the car as the journey progressed. She blessed the illuminating moonlight, but had no attention to spare for the beauty of the night, all her energies concentrated on the unfolding ribbon of road, which looped in and out of the pine-topped cliffs in relentless hairpin bends that raised beads of perspiration on her forehead, and made her palms so slippery with sweat that she was obliged to wipe a hand down the silk dress every now and then when she could bring herself to spare one from the wheel. It seemed like hours before Cabo Feliz finally came in sight, by which time it was difficult to judge which of the car's occupants was the more exhausted.

'Just park it here. I'll walk you down to the villa,' mumbled Nick, when they reached the hotel.

'No fear,' said Clem after one look at his ravaged face. 'You get out and go straight up to bed. It's only half a mile to the house. I'll drive down and leave the car parked there. You can pick it up in the morning.'

Nick protested feebly, but gave in without much struggle, quite obviously too ill to argue any more. Clem kept the engine running until he was safely inside the hotel, then drove the Mini down to the villa at a crawl and reversed the car inch by inch into the open space on the cliff-top next to Luiz's Mercedes.

Her knees were knocking like castanets as she got out, and she breathed in great thankful gulps of night air as she tried to discover which key locked the doors of the Mini. She found she could laugh a little now the journey was over, thinking it was a blessing she hadn't explained to Nick that, although she owned a current licence, driving was something she actively detested, and only the fact that he was in such dire straits had driven her to volunteer her services. By a process of elimination she found the right key at last, but before she could insert it in the lock found to her horror that the car was slowly moving backwards.

'Oh, my God!' she gasped, and yanked at the door handle, some instinct prompting her to try to get at the handbrake, but the momentum of the car defeated her, knocking her over despite its size, and by the time she scrambled to her feet all she could do was watch in utter horror as in graceful slow-motion the car slid backwards over the cliff and disappeared from view. She screamed and rushed to the edge, in time to see the Mini somersault in its fall to the pebbles below, landing upside-down with a final, sickening crash. She moaned, clutching her arms across her chest, waiting with staring eyes for the inevitable explosion. Nothing happened. She waited, teeth chattering, then raced up to the house, to collide with Luiz, who was running towards her.

'*Qué pasa?*' he demanded, putting his arms round her. '*Dios*, Clem, what happened?'

'Nick was too ill to drive back,' she panted, 'so I did. I let him off at the hotel and drove down here to park, but I couldn't have ratcheted the handbrake up properly. Oh God, Luiz, it was a hire car, and I just let it fall off the cliff!'

Charity had arrived by this time, and snatched her sister into her arms as Clem gasped out her story again while Luiz ran down to the beach.

When he returned, Luiz spread his hands, shrugging. 'I think it is a write-off, *no?*'

Clem let out a wail of despair.

'All right, all right, love. It's only a car.' Over her twin's dishevelled head Charity exchanged a look with her husband, and Luiz put an arm around both girls, and led them into the house.

It was a long time before Clem was restored to anything like normal, requiring tea and a great deal of straight talking from both Luiz and Charity before she was able to put the accident into perspective.

'*Querida,*' said Luiz earnestly, as he held her hand, 'there was no life lost, no one else involved, no one was even hurt——'

'Except Clem's hands and knees,' muttered

Charity, sponging the grazes.

'But just look at your dress, Chatty!' moaned Clem.

'Who cares about a dress?'

'And if the matter of money worries you, I am sure the insurance will cover it,' Luiz added.

'But what on earth am I going to say to Nick?' Clem put her head in her hands and groaned.

'Shall I talk to him for you?'

'No, Luiz. Please. I'll tell him myself. I'll come up to the hotel first thing, before he finds out.'

'How did you come to be driving, anyway?' demanded Charity.

Clem explained about Nick's migraine and the nightmare journey home.

'You mean you drove all the way from S'Agaro?' said Charity in awe. 'Good heavens, I think you'd better have a brandy. Llanhowell to Monmouth is usually your limit—and unless the law's changed lately, they still drive on the left over there.'

'I'll admit I was a bit nervous—no, I wasn't, I was petrified! So was Nick, I think, but he was too polite to say so. In fact he was very restrained—unless he was too ill to care.' Clem shrugged and accepted the brandy Luiz gave her. 'But since he couldn't see properly, I didn't see what else I could do.'

'You must have been shaking so much by the time you got out of the car, you weren't even capable of pulling up the handbrake properly.' Charity let out a sigh. 'Anyway, the important thing is that you're in one piece. To hell with the car!'

Clem put out a hand to cover her sister's. 'I really

am sorry, Chatty. Did the crash give you a shock?'

'No. I was just getting out of the bath when I heard a dull thud in the distance, then I went out on the balcony and saw Luiz running one way, and you the other, and I got myself down here pretty fast.'

Clem stood up. 'I'll let you get to bed. My apologies again. Frankly, I think I'd better get myself back to Putney.'

Charity protested at once, but Clem shook her head decisively.

'If anything else upsetting happens, you'll be lucky to stay pregnant, Chatty. I've caused too much commotion one way and another as it is. I'll come back to you again after the baby's born, when— when I'm a bit more sorted out.'

Whenever that was likely to be, Clem thought morosely, as she tried to get to sleep. A shower had dispelled the effects of the brandy, and the prospect of having to own up to Nick about the car next day was not a thought that wooed sleep. She dozed a little intermittently at last, but as the first rays of light lit the sky she woke up again and decided to get dressed. She pulled on shorts and a sweatshirt and crept downstairs very quietly to shut herself in the kitchen and drink cup after cup of strong tea until the day was advanced enough for her to go down to the beach.

She let herself out of the house and went down to the small cove to inspect the car in despair. It lay like a dead red beetle, wheels turned up to the sky. Luiz was right, thought Clem. It was a total write-off, even to her own inexpert eye, and she turned away disconsolately to head for the sunbeds which Pilar always pushed well up the pebbles at night. Clem slumped down on one, noticing a forgotten beach towel lying half hidden under the other bed. She picked it up and sniffed at the salt and sand dampness of it, then curled up wearily on one of the beds, huddling the towel around her like a blanket.

She dozed a little for a time, worn out by her restless night, then she jerked upright at the sound of pebbles flying as Nick's unmistakable figure hurtled down the private path to the beach. He ran like the wind towards the wrecked Mini, and Clem tore after him, calling to him hoarsely as she ran across the beach, but even before she reached him it was plain he was too frantic to hear anything. She put on a burst of speed as she saw him push frenziedly at the car, reaching him as he fell on his knees beside it, maniacal in his attempt to see inside.

Sobbing for breath, Clem touched his shoulder and he leapt to his feet, staring at her as though she were an apparition, tears pouring down his haggard face.

'I'm sorry,' she choked, and began to cry in sympathy. 'I didn't put the handbrake on properly last night, Nick.'

Nick spat something excessively vulgar about the handbrake and dragged her into his arms, kissing her feverishly, his hands running all over her body to convince himself she was all in one piece. Clem locked her arms round his neck and kissed him back, her tears mingled with his as she sobbed out an explanation which he interrupted every other word or so to kiss her again and again.

At last he thrust her away from him and held her by the elbows, shaking her hard until her teeth rattled.

'I saw the car from up there.' He jerked his head towards the cliff-top. 'I thought you were *in* it, woman! When I came running down here, it felt like the descent into hell. Stop *crying!*'

'I will if you will,' she retorted, brushing the tears from her eyes, and he stopped dead, touching one of his hands in amazement to the wetness on his face.

'See what you reduce me to!' he said wrathfully, and fell to kissing her again; hot, salt kisses fired by the violence of relief.

Clem returned them with equal ardour, clutching him to her until after a while her knees began to buckle, and she tore her mouth away long enough to gasp, 'Let's sit down!'

She led him to the sunbeds, where, careless of who might be watching from the villa, Nick drew her down to lie full length against him, holding her tightly in his arms as he kissed her mouth and nose and red, swollen eyes.

'Don't cry any more, darling,' he whispered, but the very tenderness in his voice made her tears well up again. Clem sniffed inelegantly and tried to smile.

'No one would believe it if they saw me crying, you know. Charity was always the one who cried. Once I was grown up I shed very few tears until I met you. And even then they weren't for the usual reasons.'

Nick stroked her hair back from her damp forehead, the light in his eyes making her breath catch in her throat. 'What were the reasons?'

'That night, in the moonlight in your house, when everything was still so beautiful between us, I cried because I was so happy.'

'How about afterwards?' he asked soberly. 'When everything blew up in our faces?'

'I just went sort of numb with shock when you told me you didn't want me any more——'

'Oh no, I didn't,' he corrected swiftly. 'I've never stopped wanting you.' And to prove it he began to kiss her again, caressing her with growing urgency, driven by an instinctive urge to mate after the near-brush with tragedy.

'Come up with me to my room!' he said hoarsely.

'I can't!'

'Why not?'

'I look far too much like the owner's wife!'

Nick groaned and crushed her to him so hard she feared for her ribs. 'I begin to realise the drawbacks of this twin arrangement,' he said bitterly.

'And you can't make love to me here!' Clem protested after a few ecstatic moments.

'Where can I, then? Because if I don't soon, I think I'll go insane!'

She pushed him away, staring up at him searchingly. 'Nick, is that what you want most?'

The hot urgency faded in Nick's eyes as they held hers. 'You mean you think I'm too obsessed with thoughts of possessing your body?'

'Not exactly. After—after what I witnessed just

now . . .' She trailed into silence, flushing.

'You mean when you saw me go mad because I thought you were dead?' He smiled ruefully. 'Did that convince you that maybe my feelings for you were more cerebral than you suspected?'

'Yes, it did.' She touched a hand to his face, and gave him a wicked smile. 'But the thing I find even more convincing is that you haven't said a word about the car.'

Nick grinned. 'Which demonstrates very clearly where my priorities lie, apart from all the hundreds of other reasons I shall list for you when I'm in a calmer frame of mind.' He took her face in his hands. 'Just now I experienced the worst moment of my life when I thought you might be dead—or injured. I never want to go through that again. I just can't face the thought of life without you, Clemency Vaughan. These past few weeks have been a nightmare.'

'I haven't enjoyed them overmuch myself.' She looked away, feeling oddly shy. 'So what now?'

Nick laughed in delight at her embarrassment, and put his arms round her, drawing her close. 'Before anything else happens to prevent it, I vote we get married, my darling, as soon as humanly possible.'

Clem smiled at him blissfully. 'Yes, please!'

'I'd appreciate a very early date for the wedding, Miss Vaughan, because I've just come to a very difficult decision,' he went on, sighing. 'Until we're legally and permanently bound in holy wedlock, my beautiful girl, I'm determined I'm not going to allow myself more than a few kisses and maybe a cuddle or two.'

Clem's eyes narrowed to a laughing blue gleam. 'Oh? Why?'

'As an act of faith. To prove that I want not only your unquestionably tempting body, but your company and your conversation, and, even more important, your helping hand when it comes to scraping paper off walls——'

'My what?'

'We'd better redecorate the house, don't you think?' Nick's eyes danced. 'Unless you don't like my house, of course, but I very much hope you do. For a start it really *is* mine, lock, stock and barrel, and anywhere else in the same area is bound to cost an arm and a leg. Besides which I have some very sentimental associations with that bedroom of mine. Not that you're going to share it again until we tie the knot, of course,' he added virtuously.

Clem was so inordinately pleased by this declaration of intent, she hugged him close, raining kisses on his smug face. 'That's the nicest thing any man's ever said to me!'

'The reverse, I gather, from some of the propositions you get!'

'I seem to remember a singularly unique proposition from you, Nicholas Wood, the night you saw me in innocent company with my brother.'

Nick closed his eyes, shuddering. 'The worst part of it was that I meant it. I was driven to the prospect of sharing you with other men, just so long as you included me among the number.' He shook his head violently. 'I'd never have kept to it.'

'So the offer no longer stands?' she asked, straight-faced.

He growled, his eyes glittering. 'No. Or I strangle you.'

'Persuasive argument. OK—just you, then. Which it has been from the moment we met,' she added matter-of-factly. 'I've never loved any other man, Nick, nor ever will. Only you.'

They melted together in a trembling embrace which grew prolonged and almost unbearable, until it was interrupted at last by a small, resigned voice.

'Mama says breakfast's *ready*.'

Nick released his flushed bride-to-be and grinned at the two little girls regarding them with stern disapproval. '*Hola, señoritas. Buenos dias.* Am I invited too?'

Dolly and Luiza nodded enthusiastically as Nick held out his arms to them, their brown faces glowing up as he swung one up in either arm to walk up the beach.

'Mama says you're Tío Nick now,' announced Luiza with satisfaction.

'Your uncle, eh?' Nick's eye met Clem's over the curly fair heads. 'How did Charity know that already?'

Clem shrugged. 'We're twins, remember.'

He rolled his eyes at her. 'I hope this private hotline you share is—er—selective in certain delicate areas.'

'Don't be rude!'

* * *

In the garden the moon silvered the grass and smudged in dark shadows under the bushes, but this time frost added sparkle to a lawn which was not only small and a long way from any lake, but bounded by fences and houses in one of the streets of Parson's Green. It was a cold February night, and Mr and Mrs Nicholas Wood were At Home to a large number of friends and relatives invited to celebrate the success of the best-selling novel *Flight from a Far Horizon.*

The house, newly decorated, was alive with music and laughter as Clem and Nick circulated among their guests, receiving congratulations on all sides.

'Fantastic book, Nick,' said Robina, who was a superb advertisement for her own business in a watered silk suit with an exquisite camellia on her lapel, made by her partner's unmistakable hand. 'I mean, even Oliver was enthralled by it—I couldn't get him to put it down every night in bed.'

'Then you're slipping, Robina,' said Charity, standing, as always, in the circle of her husband's arm. 'Luiz never reads in bed.'

'No,' he agreed solemnly, his grey eyes gleaming wickedly. 'I work so hard all day, my eyes refuse to stay open!' But he kissed his wife's cheek, in loving contradiction to his words.

The book had been gratifyingly well-received, but the party was by way of a housewarming, as well as a celebration, since the months since the Wood/Vaughan wedding day had been spent in redecorating the house to a standard Clem had finally pronounced satisfactory only a week or so previously.

'It's lovely, darling,' said Angharad Vaughan, who, with Kit her eldest daughter, was helping with the buffet Clem had insisted on catering for herself.

'You've got quite a flair,' agreed Kit, who was looking particularly beautiful in a black velvet dress of Clem's own design. 'You've worked wonders here in a very short time. I don't know where you get the energy to do everything you do.'

'Secret source,' said Clem, smiling as Nick appeared at her elbow, exchanged a silent look with her, smiled back in apparent satisfaction, then went off again to ply his guests with drinks after a brief word with his father-in-law.

Dr Vaughan shook his head in wonder. 'Amazing how you and Nick communicate, *cariad*. Just like you and Charity.'

Clem smiled at her twin. 'It was the acid test, I suppose.'

'Finding a man on the same wavelength,' Charity nodded, serious for a moment. 'I was lucky enough to find my man very early on in life.'

'Whereas I've been very backward at finding mine!'

A pretty girl with long, dark hair came running into the dining-room. 'Shall I start handing round some of the goodies, Clem?'

'Thanks, Melanie. Get Penry to lend a hand.' Clem smiled affectionately at Nick's young sister, and handed her a tray of canapés. 'Tear him away from whichever female he happens to be seducing.'

'Females, plural,' said Melanie, grinning. 'There's a ring of them in the conservatory, drooling over his bedside manner, but don't worry. Just leave 'em to me.'

It was a happy occasion, with a mixture of guests who hailed from many and various backgrounds, but blended happily to enjoy each other's company, only a few of the newest of the Woods' acquaintances open-mouthed when they saw Mrs Nicholas Wood and Senora Luiz Santana together for the first time. Most of the company were used to the phenomenon, but even to those who weren't there was less difficulty than usual for the time being in telling the former Vaughan twins apart.

Charity, dazzling in cobalt silk, had recovered her usual curvaceous slimness again following the birth of her son, but was easy to tell her apart from her sister for once because, although Clem's dress was exquisite, of midnight-blue pleated chiffon, with crystal beads and embroidery at the low-cut neckline, it was nevertheless a maternity dress. For the time being its clever cut concealed the fact, but nothing could conceal an extra dimension to Clemency Wood's looks on this particular evening. Her eyes shone like sapphires in her radiant face, and her hair seemed to curl about her face with a life of its own as she laughed and chatted with Nick's editor, and Nick's parents and friends, Emma and Jane and their respective escorts, flitting from one group to another like a glittering blue butterfly.

'It was a great party,' she said, yawning, after the last of the guests had finally gone. 'But I'm glad the rest of my family are staying with Kit, much as I love them all. It's good to have the place to ourselves.'

Nick sat on the edge of the bed and drew her down beside him, eyeing her in a possessive way she responded to at once, sliding her arms round his neck and bringing his dark head down to hers as she kissed him slowly and pleasurably on the mouth.

'You are so incredible,' he said huskily after a while, as he held her close. 'I could hardly take my eyes off you tonight. You seemed to be lit up like a torch, eclipsing every other woman in the room —which was no mean feat among the beauties assembled under our humble roof.'

'You mean with Chatty and Kit and Melanie and Robina——'

'To name but a few. And not one of them could hold a candle to you tonight, darling.'

'You're prejudiced!'

'Not a bit of it. Even Penry commented on it, so it must have been blindingly obvious. And your father positively bristled with pride.' Nick grinned. 'By the way, did you notice Jenny's husband? He couldn't take his eyes off you.'

Clem pulled a face and stood up, turning her back so Nick could unfasten her dress. 'Mustn't alienate your editor, darling.'

His lips touched the satin-smooth place where her neck curved into her shoulder. 'Never mind anyone else. My turn now, since we are finally, as they say, alone at last.'

'Ah yes, Nick Wood, but there's a difference. It's not just your *eyes* you can't take off me, is it?'

'Very true. I intend to take off this dress too, and this, and these—' And Nick slowly undressed her, with delicate care, until they were together in the big new bed and everyone else was forgotten in the rapture they shared together, gentler and less fierce now, in deference to the future arrival, but their loving as intense and joyous as it had been from the beginning.

'There's a moon out there,' said Clem later, smoothing the tumbled dark hair away from Nick's forehead. 'Just like there was that first night. Only it was summer, and warm then.'

'I'm not exactly cold now, sweetheart,' Nick raised his head and looked into her eyes. It's doesn't make any difference, you know. I love you in the rain and mud as well as the moonlight. All the ways there are. And other ways I'll make up as I go along.'

Clem eyed him thoughtfully. 'I'm pleased to hear it. I hope you'll love me when I'm tired and crotchety from getting up in the night, and even before that stage, when I'm what's popularly known as "great with child".'

'All the time. Always,' Nick assured her.

'Good. Because I'm going to be both with a vengeance, believe me,' she smiled at him smugly. 'I had another reason for celebrating tonight, Nick, but I wanted to keep the news until we were alone together without any interruptions.' She paused dramatically, her eyes dancing. 'Would you believe that at my check-up today they said we're going to have twins?'

He stared at her incredulously, then his eyes filled with unholy glee, and he began to laugh, hugging her to him convulsively. 'I told my mother tonight I was twice as fortunate as most men. I didn't know then just how right I was!' He raised his head to look into her radiant face in question. 'Hey, wait a minute! I thought identical twins were a freak of nature, not hereditary.'

'True.' Clem looked inordinately pleased with herself. 'I really put one over on Chatty for once, didn't I? The Vaughan brand of twin might not be hereditary, but the Wood family are about to be blessed with two little simultaneous darlings just the same.'

Nick smoothed her hair away from her face and shrugged. 'I'm not surprised, really.'

'Oh? Why?'

'It seems quite logical to have produced two babies at once, now I come to think of it.'

Clem looked up into her husband's face, intrigued. 'Go on—I'm all ears.'

'And not just ears by a long way,' he said with feeling, looking down at the picture she made in the lamplight.

'Don't wander from the point! Tell me exactly why you consider our imminent production of twins so logical?'

'Twins are a perfectly fair result, in my opinion, if one takes into account the fact that I love you twice as much as any man ever loved his woman, all the way back to——' Nick paused tantalisingly.

'When?' Clem demanded, touching a loving hand to his cheek.

He smiled down at her. 'Oh, I don't know, at a rough estimate, I suppose you could say the Garden of Eden!'

Harlequin Presents®

Coming Next Month

Available in May wherever paperback books are sold, or through Harlequin Reader Service:

In the U.S.
901 Fuhrmann Blvd.
P.O. Box 1397
Buffalo, N.Y. 14240-1397

In Canada
P.O. Box 603
Fort Erie, Ontario
L2A 5X3

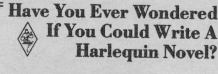

Have You Ever Wondered If You Could Write A Harlequin Novel?

Here's great news—Harlequin is offering a series of cassette tapes to help you do just that. Written by Harlequin editors, these tapes give practical advice on how to make your characters—and your story—come alive. There's a tape for each contemporary romance series Harlequin publishes.

Mail order only

All sales final

TO: *Harlequin Reader Service*
Audiocassette Tape Offer
P.O. Box 1396
Buffalo, NY 14269-1396

I enclose a check/money order payable to HARLEQUIN READER SERVICE® for $9.70 ($8.95 plus 75¢ postage and handling) for EACH tape ordered for the total sum of $_____*
Please send:

☐ Romance and Presents   ☐ Intrigue
☐ American Romance   ☐ Temptation
☐ Superromance   ☐ All five tapes ($38.80 total)

Signature_____

Name:_____
                                          (please print clearly)

Address:_____

State:_____ Zip:_____

*Iowa and New York residents add appropriate sales tax.

AUDIO-H

This April, don't miss Harlequin's new Award of
Excellence title from

Harlequin Presents...

CAROLE MORTIMER

Award of Excellence

elusive as the unicorn

*When Eve Eden discovered that Adam
Gardener, successful art entrepreneur, was
searching for the legendary English artist, The
Unicorn, she nervously shied away. The Unicorn's
true identity hit too close to home....*

*Besides, Eve was rattled by Adam's
mesmerizing presence, especially in the light
of the ridiculous coincidence of their names—
and his determination to take advantage of it!
But Eve was already engaged to marry her
longtime friend, Paul.*

*Yet Eve found herself troubled by the different
choices Adam and Paul presented. If only the
answer to her dilemma didn't keep eluding her....*

HP1258-1